This book belongs to

_____

ONCE UPON A PRINCESS

VOLUME TWO

ONCE UPON

A
PRINCESS

VOLUME TWO

New York

Stories translated from the Disney Libri series by Carin McLain

Printed in Singapore

First Edition

1 2 3 4 5 6 7 8 9 10

Library of Congress Catalog Card Number: 2002093795

ISBN: 0-7868-3466-8

For more Disney Press fun, visit www.disneybooks.com

Table of Contents

The Story of Belle 9

The Story of Pocahontas 111

The Story of Cinderella 199

THE STORY OF
Belle

A Poor Provincial Life

The day began like any other—an ordinary day, typical of life in a small French village. The local farmer pushed a cart filled with plump orange pumpkins down the street. In a second-story salon, the barber began clipping his customer's hair. The butcher's stand opened for business, and his shouts rang out through the street. The pleasant smell of fresh fruit from the fruit seller's stand filled the air. All over the village, people opened their windows, breathed in the morning air, and called a cheery *"Bonjour!"* to their neighbors.

And as she did on most ordinary days, a young woman named Belle was walking toward the market. She was carrying a basket and looking at the everyday activities going on around her.

Most of the villagers knew the pretty brown-haired girl by sight. "Good morning, Belle," the baker greeted her as she passed his shop.

"Good morning, monsieur," Belle said politely.

The baker set a tray of freshly baked bread on his windowsill. "Where are you off to?" he asked Belle.

"The bookshop," Belle replied. "I just finished the most wonderful story about a beanstalk and an ogre and a—"

"That's nice," the baker interrupted. He leaned in the shop door to shout to someone inside. "Marie! The baguettes! Hurry up!"

Belle sighed and moved on, knowing the man wasn't really interested in hearing about her book. In this country town, most people weren't interested in fairy tales or stories of adventure. Of course, Belle wasn't like most people. She loved to read about anything. There were so many interesting things going on in those books! It was too bad the same couldn't be said for her village.

Luckily, there was a small bookshop in the marketplace. The owner allowed Belle to borrow books whenever she liked.

"Good morning!" Belle greeted the shopkeeper as she entered the bookshop. "I've come to return the book I borrowed."

"Finished already?" the shop-keeper exclaimed in surprise.

"Oh, I couldn't put it down," Belle told him. "Have you got anything new?"

"Not since yester-day," the storekeeper replied with a laugh.

"That's all right." Belle climbed the

ladder leading to the higher shelves. Spotting an old favorite near the top, she grabbed it. "I'll borrow this one."

"That one?" The shopkeeper peered at the cover through his spectacles. "But you've read it twice!"

"Well, it's my favorite!" Belle exclaimed. "Far-off places, daring sword fights, magic spells, a prince in disguise . . ."

The shopkeeper chuckled, charmed as always by Belle's enthusiasm. "If you like it all that much, it's yours! I insist!"

"Thank you, thank you very much!" Belle could hardly believe her good fortune. She and her father, Maurice, didn't have much money—her father was an inventor whose inventions only rarely worked—and so the gift of a book was something special.

Bidding farewell to the shopkeeper, Belle carried her new book out to the town square. As she wandered through the streets, her mind was far away. At first, she thought of the book she'd finished the night before, and then of the new one tucked in her basket.

Then her thoughts turned to her mother, who had died when Belle was a little girl. It was through her mother that Belle had come by her love of reading. Every night before bed, Belle's mother would come to her daughter's room. Sometimes she would bring a book she'd borrowed. At other times, she would spin stories out of her own imagination. Even in those days they hadn't had much money. But they had always been happy. As soon as Belle was old enough, her mother had taught her daughter to read so that she could enjoy books on her own.

Soon after that, Belle's mother had taken ill and died. Belle and her father still missed her every day. But at least Belle could remember her through her own love of reading. Every time she read a new story, she imagined what her mother would think of it. That helped keep her mother's memory alive, just as much as the portrait sitting on Belle's dresser at home.

A MOST PECULIAR GIRL

Sitting on the edge of the fountain in the town square, Belle turned through the familiar pages of her new book. She could hardly believe it belonged to her. She paused at her favorite part—the chapter in which the heroine meets her Prince Charming. It was such a wonderful story!

But she didn't have time to sit and read it just then. She wanted to get home to see how her father's latest invention was going. He had high hopes for this one. If he finished it in time, he

would be able to enter it in the fair being held
the next day in a larger town a few miles away.

Still thinking about her book, she wandered
back through town toward home. Partway there, a
tall, handsome man dressed in hunting clothes
jumped out in front of her.

"Hello, Belle," Gaston greeted her.

"*Bonjour*, Gaston," Belle replied politely. She
didn't care much for Gaston—in her opinion he

was vain, shallow, and silly, much more interested in improving his muscles than his mind. But that was no reason to be rude to the young man.

She prepared to move on, but Gaston had other ideas. Snatching the book out of her hands, he peered at it suspiciously.

"Gaston," Belle said with annoyance, "may I have my book, please?"

"How can you read this?" Gaston exclaimed. "There are no pictures!"

"Well, some people use their imagination." Belle couldn't help being amused by Gaston's simple-mindedness.

"Belle, it's about time you got your head out of those books and paid attention to more important things," Gaston declared, tossing the book into a mud puddle. "Like me!"

It was no secret that Gaston was interested in Belle. She was the prettiest girl in the village, and in Gaston's mind that made her the best. And he was sure that if anyone deserved the best, it was he! All

the other girls in the village swooned every time the handsome hunter walked by. Belle, however, seemed completely indifferent to his good looks. That only made Gaston all the more determined to win her over.

"The whole town is talking about it," Gaston went on as Belle knelt down to retrieve her book and wipe off the mud. "It's not right for a woman to read! Soon she starts getting ideas, and thinking. . . ."

"Gaston," Belle said, "you are positively primeval!"

Not realizing he'd been insulted, Gaston smiled. "Why, thank you, Belle! What do you say you and me take a walk over to the tavern and take a look at my trophies?"

"Maybe some other time," Belle replied.

Ignoring her refusal, Gaston put an arm around Belle and steered her in the direction of the tavern. Gaston was so unaccustomed to hearing anyone say no to him that he often didn't bother to take notice when someone did.

"Please, Gaston, I can't!" Belle managed to pull away after a few steps. "I have to get home to help my father. Good-bye."

Gaston's best friend, LeFou, stepped forward with a laugh. He had been watching the whole exchange.

"That crazy old loon?" he exclaimed at Belle's mention of her father. "He needs all the help he can get!"

Gaston laughed along with his friend. But Belle whirled around with an angry expression on her pretty face.

"Don't talk about my father that way!" she cried. "My father is not crazy! He's a genius!"

The blast of an explosion coming from the direction of her father's workshop interrupted any further discussion. Ignoring the two men's laughter, Belle ran for home.

When she got there, smoke was billowing everywhere. "Papa?" Belle called, coughing, as she entered the house and went down to the workshop. "Are you all right?"

"I'm about ready to give up on this hunk of junk!" Maurice cried in frustration.

Belle smiled, relieved to see that nothing was really wrong.

"You always say that," she reminded her father fondly.

"I mean it this time!" Maurice insisted. "I'll never get this boneheaded con-traption to work!"

"Yes, you will," Belle assured him. "And you'll win first prize at the fair tomorrow. And become a world-famous inventor."

Maurice glanced at her. "You really believe that?"

Belle smiled at him. "I always have."

"Well, what are we waiting for?" Maurice asked, his good spirits revived, as always, by his daughter's support. "I'll have this thing fixed in no time!" He hurried back over to his invention. Belle stood by to hand him the tools he needed. "So, did you have a good time in town today?" he asked her.

"I got a new book," Belle said. But she wasn't really thinking about that. "Papa," she said uncertainly, "do you think I'm odd?"

"My daughter—odd?" Maurice exclaimed. "Where would you get an idea like that?"

"Oh, I don't know." Belle sighed, thinking of the conversation she had had earlier with Gaston. "It's just that I'm not sure I fit in here. There's no one I can really talk to."

"What about that Gaston?" Maurice asked as he fiddled with his invention. "He's a handsome fellow."

"He's handsome, all right," Belle said. "And rude, and conceited! Oh, Papa, he's not for me."

"Well, don't you worry," Maurice told her, "because this invention's going to be the start of a new life for us. I think that's done it." Making one last adjustment, he stood up. "Let's give it a try."

With a whir and a whistle, the invention came to life. Within moments it had chopped a log into firewood and tossed it neatly into a stack by the wall.

"It works!" Belle cried with delight.

"It does?" Maurice sounded surprised, then joyful. "It does!"

"You did it!" Belle exclaimed proudly, giving him a quick hug as more firewood flew through the air. "You really did it!"

Maurice asked Belle to hitch up his horse, Phillipe. "I'm off to the fair!" he declared.

Soon Belle was waving good-bye as her father  rode off with his invention in tow. She watched until he was out of sight, then wandered back inside. She wondered if her father was right. Would this invention really change their lives? Maybe now they would be able to get out of this sleepy little town and see the world!

In the meantime, she decided it was the perfect

moment to read her book. She went inside and picked it up.

For an hour or two, she was able to read in peace. Then there was a knock at the door. Belle looked up in surprise. Who could that be? She and her father didn't get many visitors.

Leaving her book open on the table, she walked over and checked the viewing tube—another of her father's inventions. It allowed her to see who was standing outside.

To her dismay, the tube showed her Gaston's smug yet handsome face. What in the world did *he* want?

Before she could decide what to do, Gaston pulled the door open and stepped inside. "Gaston!" Belle exclaimed. "What a pleasant surprise."

She didn't sound very convincing, but Gaston didn't seem to notice. Instead of wearing his usual hunting attire, he was dressed in a fancy coat and a jaunty tie.

"I'm just full of surprises," he said. "You know, Belle, there's not a girl in town who wouldn't love to be in your shoes. This is the day your dreams come true!"

"What do you know about my dreams, Gaston?" Belle asked with a rueful smile.

"Plenty!" Gaston assured her. He sat down in a chair beside the fireplace, comfortably propping his

muddy boots on the table—right on top of Belle's book. "Picture this: a rustic hunting lodge, my latest kill roasting on the fire . . ." He kicked off his boots, wriggling his toes. "And my little wife massaging my feet . . ."

Belle didn't try to hide her distaste as she stared at Gaston's ugly feet.

". . . while the little ones play on the floor with the dogs," he went on. "We'll have six or seven."

"Dogs?" Belle asked, still distracted at the thought of what Gaston was proposing.

"No, Belle," Gaston corrected. "Strapping boys, like me!"

"Imagine that," Belle said. Gaston had stood up by now, and Belle grabbed her muddy book and set it on the shelf before he could do any more damage to it. She had put up with just about enough of Gaston and his arrogance and self-centeredness. How could he assume that she would want to go along with his plans? It was obvious that he didn't understand her at all. And that was just as well, because she certainly didn't understand *him*!

Still, he kept talking. "And do you know who that little wife will be?" he asked teasingly.

"Let me think," Belle said nervously.

But Gaston wasn't interested in waiting for her to figure it out. "You, Belle!" he announced in reply to his own question. He leaned toward her, obviously expecting a thrilled response.

Belle slipped away. "Gaston, I'm—I'm—speechless!" She leaned against the front door, trying not to laugh out loud at the thought of marrying the crude hunter. "I really don't know what to say."

Gaston stepped toward her, leaning both hands against the door above her shoulders. "Say you'll marry me."

Belle gazed up at him. "I'm very sorry, Gaston," she said, feeling for the doorknob as Gaston pursed his lips and prepared to kiss her. "But—but—I just don't deserve you!"

And with that, she turned the doorknob and

stepped back. Gaston's weight pushed the door open, and he tumbled out, head over heels. "Whoa!" he cried as he splashed into a mud puddle outside.

Belle shut the door again quickly. She knew that Gaston had a temper, and she didn't want to face it right now. She was too annoyed herself.

Just imagine! A man like Gaston thinking that Belle would thank him for the chance to become his wife. It was outrageous. Preposterous. And it was just like Gaston to expect such a thing.

No, Belle had no intention of spending the rest of her life cooking and cleaning for that boorish, brainless man and taking care of a whole brood of wild children who took after their obnoxious father. She had much bigger dreams than that.

Including one very special dream . . .

SOMEDAY . . .

Belle couldn't help thinking back to something that had happened when she was young. It was just a year or two after her mother had died, soon after Maurice had moved their little family to the village. Belle had been thrilled the first time her father had taken her for a walk into the center of town. Everything was so different, so exciting!

"Look at this, Papa!" she had cried, racing ahead of him. She pointed to the fruit seller's stand—so many kinds of apples! And then to the fishmonger's

stand—all the different types of fish! To young Belle, life in this new town seemed wonderful.

It was a beautiful day in early spring. The villagers had smiled upon seeing the little girl's enthusiasm.

"What a pretty child!" A woman cooed, bending over to give Belle a pat on the head.

The woman's friend leaned toward Maurice as he hurried up to them, huffing and puffing from trying to keep up with his daughter. "You'd better keep a close eye on your little girl," she warned. "The gypsies are in town."

"Gypsies?" Belle cried with delight. "Mama read me a story about gypsies. They can see into the future!"

"Now, now, Belle," Maurice said with a chuckle, taking her by the hand. "That was just a story. Nobody can see the future."

The village women smiled and moved off. "Be careful," one of them called over her shoulder as Maurice and Belle continued on their way.

"Papa, can we go see the gypsies?" Belle begged, tugging on her father's arm. "Please, Papa?"

Maurice looked worried. "Well, I don't know, Belle," he said. "I'm not sure we should—ah!" Suddenly distracted, he pointed. "Look, Belle, a hardware shop! I'd better go see what sort of parts I'll be able to buy here for my inventions. Come along now."

Belle followed him into the shop. But she soon grew bored and restless. All there was to look at it in the hardware shop were bolts and hammers and rope. Through the window, she caught sight of a flash of bright color outside. What was that?

Slipping away toward the door, she glanced at her father. He was busy examining ax blades with the shopkeeper. Surely, he wouldn't mind if she just stepped outside for a moment. . . .

She was so busy looking over her shoulder that

she tripped over the door frame and fell right into a woman passing outside.

"Well, hello, little one," the woman said with a laugh.

"Oh, I'm sorry!" Belle gasped, righting herself and looking up into the broad, smiling face of a gypsy woman.

The gypsy laughed, making her golden hoop earrings jingle. "Don't fret, my child," she said kindly. "Such a little one as you could fall on me all day long without so much as ruffling my skirts."

Belle stared at the woman, fascinated. She looked so different, so interesting! "Can you see the future?" Belle blurted out.

The gypsy laughed again. "Well, now," she replied. "Why don't we just see about that? Give me your hand, child."

Feeling a little nervous, Belle held out her hand. What would the gypsy tell her? Would she predict a life of adventure and romance?

The gypsy peered down at Belle's little palm. "Ah,"

she said wisely. "You will live a long and happy life. But it will not always be easy. You will experience much adventure."

"Really?" Belle's eyes shone. "Adventure? That sounds wonderful!"

The gypsy gazed at her. "Remember this, my child," she said seriously. "Adventure is where you find it, and the true spirit of adventure lives only within your own heart. You must let it out by opening your mind."

Belle shivered. Hearing about the future was so exciting! "Tell me more," she begged.

The gypsy chuckled. "All right then, let's see." She looked at Belle's palm again. "Hmm, what's this?" she murmured, leaning over for a better view. "Odd. I've never seen this before. . . ."

"What? What is it?" Belle asked breathlessly.

"It looks like—well, it is a pattern that represents a castle," the gypsy said. "A great, gleaming castle of spires and towers. But the only castle like that around here is—"

"Belle!" Maurice's voice interrupted. He raced out of the shop and pulled her away from the

gypsy. "There you are! You scared me half to death. Didn't I tell you to stay in the shop?"

"I'm sorry, Papa," Belle said, still thinking about what the gypsy had just said. "But listen! This lady was just telling me the most wonderful . . ."

Her words trailed off as she turned around. The gypsy had disappeared!

She convinced her father to search for her fortune-telling friend. They checked throughout the town, but the gypsy woman was nowhere to be found. Belle was left to wonder what else the woman might have said about her future.

Ever since that day, Belle had thought often about the gypsy's words. She thought about them again now as she ran away from the house toward a broad, grassy meadow with a stunning view of the river. There was a whole world of adventure out

there—she knew it. But here in her village, the only sense of adventure seemed to be in her heart, as the gypsy had said. There was certainly nothing exciting or new to be found in the everyday happenings of the village and its people. Even the feathery seeds of a dandelion blowing in the breeze seemed to have more adventures than Belle.

Someday I will go exploring, too, Belle told herself firmly. Someday I will have a life full of adventure. Then she sighed. Of course, it would be nice to have someone to share it all with, someone who really understands how I feel. . . .

A shrill neigh interrupted her thoughts. Glancing up, she was startled to see Phillipe racing toward her, still pulling her father's invention behind him. The horse's eyes were wide open and he seemed terrified.

And Maurice was nowhere in sight.

BELLE'S SACRIFICE

Belle hurried to the horse, taking him by the bridle and trying to calm him down. "Where's Papa? Where is he, Phillipe?" she cried. "What happened?"

Phillipe continued to stomp his hooves and shake with fear. Belle wished the horse could speak, to tell her what had happened to Maurice. What if there had been an accident?

She quickly unhooked the horse's harness and leaped onto his back. "We have to find him. You have to take me to him!"

Belle rode a good distance through the forest. The farther they got from the village, the darker it seemed to get. Then they reached a section where the trees were gnarled and shrouded in fog. Finally, Phillipe carried Belle to a huge iron gate set into a high stone wall. Beyond, Belle could see the twisted, dark outline of a huge castle.

"What is this place?" Belle murmured, staring at the castle with a twinge of fear.

Phillipe seemed more nervous than ever. Letting

out another snort, he started to rear up and back away.

"Phillipe, please, steady!" She soothed him. "Steady."

As Belle slid down from the saddle, she noticed something lying on the ground just inside the castle gates. She gasped as she recognized her father's hat.

"Papa!" she cried, pushing open the gate and grabbing the hat. She stared at it for a moment, then turned her gaze up to the forbidding castle. Could her father be in there?

Belle gulped, knowing she had to go inside. She took a deep breath and headed toward the castle. She crossed the drawbridge and soon reached the enormous front door. She pushed it open and peered inside.

"Hello? Is there anyone here?" Belle called.

A deep silence lingered in the vast, dark entrance way. The castle appeared to be completely deserted. "Hello?" Belle asked again.

Still, there was no answer. But Belle wasn't going to give up until she was sure that her father wasn't

trapped somewhere inside. She stepped toward the grand staircase at the back of the hall, and walked up the musty red-carpeted stairs.

"Papa? Are you here?" she cried.

The castle was spooky. Every footstep echoed, and Belle had the eerie feeling that she was being watched. But her concern for her father overcame her fear. She continued to search, moving up one cavernous hallway and down another, calling for her father all the while.

Finally, Belle reached the foot of a winding staircase leading into one of the high towers. Peering up the stairs, she spotted the glow of candlelight and heard a muffled sound, like that of moving feet.

"Hello?" she called, excited. Perhaps someone was here after all. Perhaps it was someone who knew where her father was! "Is someone here? I'm looking for my father!"

Belle climbed up the stairs. But soon she reached a nook, where a candle was burning, unattended.

Aside from the candle's flickering flames, there was no sign or sound of life.

"That's funny," she murmured under her breath. "I'm sure there was someone." She raised her voice. "Is anyone here?"

"Belle?" a weak but familiar voice replied from somewhere just above.

"Papa!" Belle raced up the last few steps. A torch was burning in a wall sconce, and she grabbed it as she passed, kneeling beside a barred cell.

Maurice reached out a hand toward her. He was lying on the cold stone floor, looking frightened and miserable. "How did you find me?" he asked with a gasp.

"Oh, your hands are like ice!" Belle exclaimed as her father coughed. "We have to get you out of there!"

"Belle, I want you to leave this place!" Though still weak, Maurice's voice was urgent. "No time to explain. You must go. Now!"

"I won't leave you!" Belle cried.

At that moment, a strong hand clamped down on

her shoulder, pulling her away from the cell. Belle's torch went out as it tumbled to the floor. "What are you doing here?" a deep voice said with a growl.

"Who's there?" Belle cried. "Who are you?"

"The master of this castle," the voice replied from the shadows.

"I've come for my father," Belle said as bravely as she could manage. She peered into the darkness in the direction of the growling voice, but all she could see was a huge, shadowy mass. "Please, let him out. Can't you see he's sick?"

"Then he shouldn't have trespassed here!" The master of the castle roared back angrily. "He's my prisoner."

Belle argued with him, but soon she could see it would do no good. She knew what she had to do.

"Take me instead," she offered.

This time, the voice sounded surprised. "You would take his place?"

"Belle, no!" Maurice cried. "You don't know what you're doing!"

But Belle had made up her mind. "If I did, would you let him go?" she asked.

"Yes," the dark figure agreed. "But you must promise to stay here forever."

Forever? Belle gulped. What was she agreeing to, anyway? Who was this mysterious master of the castle? "Come into the light," she told him.

The figure hesitated. After a moment, he stepped forward into some light coming through a high, narrow window. Belle gasped in horror at the sight—an enormous, hideous beast!

"No, Belle!" Maurice cried. "I won't let you do this!"

That reminded Belle what was at stake—her dear father's life. She rose to her feet and approached the Beast. "You have my word," she told him.

"Done!" the Beast shouted.

Belle buried her face in her hands. What had she gotten herself into?

Meanwhile, the Beast dragged Maurice out of his cell. Maurice tried to convince Belle to change her mind. But before they could say more than a few desperate words to each other, the Beast pulled Maurice away.

"Wait!" Belle cried, but it was too late. She collapsed on the floor, sobbing. So much for her life of adventure! The rest of her life would be spent in this cold, gloomy cell.

A moment later, the Beast returned. He had just sent Maurice back to the village in his coach.

"You didn't even let me say good-bye!" Belle cried. "I'll never see him again, and I didn't get to say good-bye." She broke down into sobs.

The Beast didn't respond for a moment. Finally he spoke. "I'll show you to your room."

"My room?" Belle glanced up at him, confused. "But I thought—"

"You want to stay in the tower?" the Beast demanded. When Belle shook her head, he turned toward the staircase. "Then follow me."

He led Belle through the dim corridors of the castle. After a few minutes of silence, the Beast cleared his throat and spoke.

"The castle is your home now, so you can go any-where you like," he said. "Except the West Wing."

"What's in the West Wing?" Belle asked.

"It's forbidden!" the Beast roared.

Soon they reached a door. The Beast opened it and showed Belle inside. "If you need anything, my servants will attend you," he said as Belle stepped into her bedroom and looked around. "You will join me for dinner," he added. "That's *not* a request!" And with that, he slammed the door.

Belle collapsed onto the bed, feeling as if her heart would break. How could she spend the rest of her life here, the prisoner of that horrible, hateful beast? And would she ever see her beloved father again? After a few minutes, a knock on the door and a cheery voice interrupted Belle's sobs.

"It's Mrs. Potts, dear! I thought you might like a spot of tea."

Belle gasped as a plump little teapot hopped into the room. She was so startled that she backed into a wardrobe.

"Careful!" the wardrobe sang out in a friendly voice.

Belle could hardly believe what she was seeing and hearing. There

was Cogsworth, the mantel clock, who was the head of the household. Lumiere, the candelabrum, was the butler. Mrs. Potts, the teapot, and her son, Chip, the teacup, served in the kitchen. Even the castle's dog had been changed into a friendly, tassel-wagging foot-stool.

Meeting the kind, enchanted objects made Belle feel a little better. But she still had no intention of sitting down to dinner with the Beast who had imprisoned her.

The Beast was irate when he heard of her decision. "If she doesn't eat with me," he said, growling at the servants, "then she doesn't eat at all!"

A few hours later, Belle's stomach started to rumble. She decided to slip out of her room and look for something to eat. It didn't take her long to find the kitchen. Though Cogsworth was worried about defying the master's orders, Mrs. Potts,

Lumiere, and the others soon had all the kitchen objects working hard to fix Belle a delicious meal. They even sang and danced to entertain her while she ate.

As she finished the last course, Belle felt better than she had since coming to the castle. She decided to do a little exploring. Slipping away from Cogsworth and Lumiere, she crept up the staircase to the West Wing. What was there that the Beast

didn't want her to
see? She couldn't help
being curious.

She found her way
to a large, dark room
with a balcony. It had
once been beautifully
furnished, but now it
was a mess. There
was a painting on the
wall of a handsome
young man. It

appeared to have been ripped to shreds by huge
claws. Had the Beast done that?

Belle stared at it for a moment, but then a

strange reddish glow caught
her eye. She turned and
moved toward it. At the
far end of the room, a
door opened onto a
balcony. Just in front of

the door was a table, and on that table stood a glass jar set over a beautiful, glowing red rose. The flower seemed to hang in midair as if by magic.

Stepping closer, Belle stared in awe. What was it? She lifted the jar for a better look.

At that moment, there was a roar of fury from behind Belle. Oh, no! The Beast had caught her snooping!

A Close Call

"Why did you come here?" the Beast growled, covering the red rose with its glass container and hunching over it protectively. "I warned you never to come here!"

"I—I'm sorry! I didn't mean any harm!" Belle stammered. As the Beast roared and started smashing things, Belle turned and raced for the door. His angry voice followed her all the way down the hall.

"Get out!" he howled.

Belle was terrified by the Beast's anger. She

raced for the front door, passing Cogsworth and Lumiere in the hall.

"Where are you going?" Lumiere cried.

"Promise or no promise, I can't stay here another minute!" Belle replied.

"Wait, please wait!" Cogsworth exclaimed.

But Belle didn't hesitate. She ran out through the door and found Phillipe in the stable. Moments later, they were galloping through the snow away from the castle.

It was past midnight, and the woods were dark and filled with shadows. After a while, Belle noticed nervously that some of the shadows seemed to be moving, even following her. She swallowed hard. Was she imagining things?

Then several sets of yellow eyes blinked into view, glowing in the dark of the underbrush. Belle gasped in horror as the creatures stepped forward into a clearing—wolves!

Phillipe reared up in panic as the wolves stalked toward him. Turning around, he ran for his life.

Belle clung to Phillipe's mane as he galloped through the snow with the wolf pack snapping at his heels. For a moment the two seemed to be out-running the pack, and Belle dared to hope that they might escape.

But several wolves had run ahead on another trail. As Phillipe crested a hill, some of the wolves darted out in front of him. Others were still coming from behind. They were surrounded!

As the horse reared up in terror, Belle was flung from the saddle. She dropped the reins, which got tangled up in the branches of a tree, so Phillipe couldn't move. The panicky horse kicked out at the wolves as Belle crawled to her feet. Grabbing a stout branch from the ground, she rushed to the horse's side and prepared to defend them both.

But as she glanced around, her heart sank. There

were so many wolves! How could she fight them all? It seemed hopeless.

Just as a wolf leaped at her, a roar rang out, louder than the growls of the wolves. A strong arm reached out and grabbed the wolf that was attacking Belle.

Belle gasped. It was the Beast! He must have followed her from the castle!

She watched fearfully as he fought the wolf pack. The animals attacked him fiercely, ripping at his

cloak and fur. But finally he overwhelmed them.
Soon he had sent the last of them whimpering and
fleeing into the night.

But the fight had taken all the Beast had. With a
groan, he staggered and collapsed to the ground,
unconscious.

Belle was already standing at Phillipe's side,
ready to get back on. She paused, glancing back at
the fallen Beast. For a moment she was tempted to

climb into the saddle and continue her ride toward home—and her father. With the wolves on the run, there would be nothing to stop her.

But she couldn't do it. She had no idea why the Beast had fought so hard to save her, but she couldn't leave him there to die.

She walked to his side and removed her cloak to place it over him. Then she led Phillipe toward the Beast's still body. It wasn't easy, but between the two of them they managed to hoist the still, heavy Beast over the saddle.

Then they began the long, slow trudge through the snow back toward the castle.

When they arrived, the servants helped carry the Beast into the parlor, where he soon regained consciousness in front of a roaring fire. Meanwhile, Mrs. Potts and the others had brought hot water and bandages so that Belle could clean the master's many wounds.

Belle dipped a bandage in the hot water and squeezed it out. Looking up, she saw the Beast licking a deep scratch on his arm. "Don't do that," she chided. Ignoring the Beast's growl, she reached for his arm. "Just hold still. . . ."

The Beast roared in pain as the hot cloth touched his wound. "That hurts!" he bellowed so loudly that the servants took a step back.

But Belle didn't move away. "If you'd hold still, it wouldn't hurt as much!" she scolded him. After

what she'd just been through in the forest, somehow the Beast's shouts didn't scare her as much as they had before.

The Beast scowled at her. "Well, if you hadn't run away, this wouldn't have happened!"

"If you hadn't frightened me, I wouldn't have run away!" Belle retorted.

"Well, you shouldn't have been in the West Wing!" the Beast cried.

"Well, you should learn to control your temper!" Belle exclaimed.

For a moment, the two of them stared at each other stubbornly. Mrs. Potts, Lumiere, and Cogsworth glanced at one another in amazement. No one had ever dared to address the master that way!

When she spoke again, Belle sounded calmer. "Now hold still," she told the Beast. "This might sting a little."

Once again, she touched the hot cloth to the Beast's wound. He clenched his teeth in pain, but this time he kept quiet and still and let Belle do her doctoring.

Belle glanced up at him, realizing there was something she needed to say. "By the way," she said, "thank you for saving my life."

The Beast was surprised for a moment. Then he nodded, his expression softening slightly.

"You're welcome," he replied.

A Special Surprise

After a few days had passed, Belle found herself wondering why she had ever been afraid of the Beast. It was true that his looks were strange and frightening and his manners were a bit rough. But underneath the gruff exterior, he was also kind and curious and intelligent—even rather sweet.

One morning, he took her by the arm. "Belle, there's something I want to show you," he told her gently. He led her to a tall door in a part of the castle she hadn't explored yet. But before they entered, he turned toward her and said, "First, you have to close your eyes. It's a surprise."

Belle closed her eyes with a smile, wondering what he had in mind. She heard the door swing open, then felt his hands take hers as he led her forward.

"Can I open them yet?" she asked.

"No, not yet," he replied.

The Beast moved away, and Belle heard the sound of heavy drapes being pulled back. Even with her eyes closed, she could tell that the room had suddenly been filled with light.

"Now can I open them?" She had grown quite curious.

"All right," the Beast said—"now!"

Belle opened her eyes—and gasped in wonder. It was a library! An enormous, glorious, beautiful library filled with more books than she had ever

seen! Shelves stretched up to the ceiling high above, and tall, narrow windows illuminated the countless volumes that filled the room. Ladders and spiral staircases allowed access to the uppermost shelves.

Belle spun around, amazed and overwhelmed. She had never dreamed there would be so many books in the whole world! The contents of the little village bookshop would have fit into the smallest corner of the vast room.

"I can't believe it," she murmured. "I've never seen so many books in all my life."

"You—you like it?" the Beast asked.

"It's wonderful!" Belle cried.

"Then it's yours," the Beast told her.

"Oh!" Belle's head spun as she tried to take in the whole room. "Thank you so much!"

Slowly, the two of them were becoming friends. They were beginning to discover the joy of being together, and sharing things with each other. It was now pleasant for Belle to walk with the Beast in the snow-covered castle garden or go for a sleigh ride in the wintry forest. That first day, she never would have imagined that she would now be able to joke with him, that they could laugh so much together. The  enormous beast was so comical when he timidly held out his paw to feed the little birds in the garden. They didn't fear his horrible claws in the least, and neither did she—at least, not anymore.

And so their daily life continued happily, each day fading into the next. Belle realized she was actually quite content at the castle. The only thing she regretted was not knowing how her father was. She knew he must miss her terribly, as she missed him. If only she could see him again!

Still, she never regretted the promise she had made, especially now that the Beast had become so dear to her. And when he invited her to a special formal dinner, she accepted gladly.

On the big day, Belle dressed carefully with help from Wardrobe. They chose a lovely golden gown that set off her beautiful brown eyes and hair. When she came out of her room and walked down to the first landing of the staircase, she looked up. The Beast was standing there, gazing down at her.

She was a little startled by how handsome he looked. He was dressed in a dashing blue jacket with gold piping that matched her dress. His fur was clean and neat, and his gaze was hopeful and a little shy.

She smiled and took his arm as he reached her. They walked down the stairs together as music started to play. The servants had arranged every-thing to make the evening special—music, candle-light, and a delicious dinner. Belle and the Beast sat together at the dining table, enjoying their food and conversation.

As she finished eating, Belle was overcome by a

sudden urge. The music was so melodic, everything was so wonderful—she just couldn't resist. Pushing back her chair, she hurried over and took the Beast by the arm, asking him to dance.

He seemed surprised but pleased. Offering his arm once again, he led her into a grand ballroom. Glass doors all around offered a glorious view of the night sky filled with stars.

They danced. The music swelled around them, and Belle could feel her heart swelling, too. Being with the Beast made her so happy. Was this friendship, or was there something more

happening between them? She smiled, not certain of the answer. But there was plenty of time to figure it out.

When they were tired of dancing, the two walked out onto the terrace. The soft glow of the twinkling stars lit Belle's face as she gazed out at the night.

"Belle," the Beast addressed her uncertainly, taking her hands in his. "Are you happy here with me?"

"Yes," Belle responded immediately. But a moment later she glanced down, her contented expression turning a bit sad.

"What is it?" the Beast asked.

Belle hesitated only a moment before telling him the truth. "If only I could see my father again," she said. "Just for a moment. I miss him so much."

The Beast hated to see the pain in her eyes as she thought of her father. He had put that pain there by accepting her imprisonment in exchange for Maurice's. He couldn't quite regret the decision, as that was how he and Belle had come to know each other. Still, he wished he could do something to help her now.

Suddenly, he realized there *was* something he could do. The enchantress who had transformed him into a beast had left him with a couple of things. One was the magic rose—if he didn't learn to love another and earn her love in return by the time the last petal fell, he would be doomed to remain a monster forever. For a while he had been certain that the spell could never be broken. But lately, he had dared to hope that Belle might be the one to break it and change him and his servants back to their human forms.

The other item the enchantress had left behind was a magic mirror. For the many long years of his enchantment, it had been the Beast's only link to

the outside world. All he had to do was command it to show him something, anything, and that person, thing, or place would appear in the mirror's face.

"There is a way," the Beast told Belle softly.

He led her upstairs and picked up the mirror. Handing it to her, he explained, "This mirror will show you anything—anything you wish to see."

Belle stared at the mirror. Her own face stared back. Could it really work?

"I'd like to see my father, please," she told the mirror uncertainly.

The mirror glowed and sparkled. A moment later, instead of Belle's own reflection, the mirror showed a most upsetting scene.

Belle gasped as she recognized her father. He was lost in the forest, staggering weakly through the snow. He was coughing and she could see him fall to his knees.

"Papa!" Belle cried in dismay. "Oh, no! He's sick! He may be dying! And he's all alone!"

The Beast turned away when he heard the anguish in her voice. He gazed down at the magic rose, noticing that another petal had dropped. He caressed the glass jar, knowing that it wouldn't be long now. . . .

But he couldn't stand to

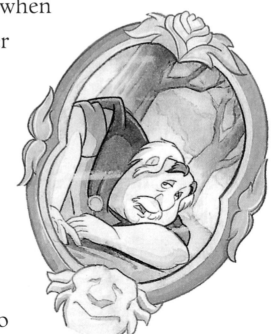

let Belle suffer a moment longer. Even if it meant sacrificing his own dreams, he must help her if he could. And he knew what he had to do.

"Then you must go to him," the Beast said.

His voice was so soft that Belle wasn't sure she'd heard him right. "What did you say?" she asked.

"I release you," the Beast said. "You are no longer my prisoner."

"You mean I'm free?" Belle was amazed. She had long since accepted that she would be here in the castle forever. But now the Beast was releasing her from that sentence so she could help her father. "Oh, thank you!" she told him, hoping he could hear in her voice how grateful she was for his kindness. "Hold on, Papa," she called out to the image in the mirror, even though she knew he couldn't hear her. "I'm on my way!"

She started to hand the mirror back to the Beast, but he pushed it gently away. "Take it with you," he said. "So you'll always have a way to look back and remember me."

"Thank you for understanding how much he needs me," Belle whispered, overcome with emotion. Now that she was free to go, she realized she had no desire to leave the Beast at all.

But she had to go. She had to save her father. Touching the Beast on the cheek, she turned away.

THE MAGIC MIRROR

Belle and Phillipe rode deep into the forest. The magic mirror guided the way, and it didn't take Belle long to find her father. She was just in time—he was lying unconscious in the snow, almost frozen.

Bundling him up, she helped him onto Phillipe and started for home. Soon she had him tucked into bed in their little cottage. With her tender care, he quickly regained consciousness.

"Belle!" he cried, hardly daring to believe it was really his beloved daughter looking down at him.

"It's all right, Papa," she assured him gently, dabbing his feverish face with a cool cloth. "I'm home."

"I thought I'd never see you again!" Maurice exclaimed.

Belle embraced him. "I missed you so much!"

"But the Beast!" Maurice suddenly remembered everything that had happened. "How did you escape?"

"I didn't escape, Papa," Belle told him. "He let me go. He's different now. He's . . . changed somehow."

She couldn't find quite the right words to

explain. Before she could think about it anymore, she heard a noise behind her. Glancing back, she saw Chip the teacup, popping out of her bag.

"Hi!" he said a bit sheepishly.

Belle laughed. "Oh! A stowaway!" she exclaimed.

Maurice laughed. "Why, hello there, little fella," he said, remembering how the little cup and his mother had been kind to him during his imprisonment. "Didn't think I'd see you again!"

Chip turned to Belle. "Belle, why did you go away?" he asked. "Don't you like us anymore?"

"Oh, Chip." Belle chuckled kindly. "Of course I do. It's just that—"

Before she could finish explaining, there was a knock on the door. Leaving Chip with her father, she went to answer it. Who could it be at this late hour?

Outside, she found a thin, pale old man with long white hair and an unpleasant expression. "May I help you?" she asked uncertainly.

"I've come to collect your father," the man said.
"Don't worry, mademoiselle. We'll take good care of
him."

The man stepped aside so Belle could see his
carriage parked out front. It was the carriage from
the local asylum.

Belle gasped. "My father's not crazy!" she
protested.

Suddenly, Gaston's friend LeFou stepped into

view. "He was raving like a lunatic!" he cried. "We all heard him, didn't we?"

Belle realized a crowd had been gathering beside the carriage. They cheered in agreement.

"No!" Belle cried. "I won't let you!"

Maurice had heard the commotion. He got out of bed and came to the front door. LeFou spotted him right away.

"Maurice!" he cried. "Tell us again, old man. Just how big was the Beast?"

As Maurice described the Beast, the crowd laughed in disbelief. Belle couldn't believe this was happening. They all thought her father was crazy. But he was telling the truth!

Before Belle knew what was happening, two orderlies stepped out of the carriage, grabbed Maurice, and dragged him away. "No!" Belle shouted. "You can't do this!" But she was powerless to stop them.

Suddenly, Gaston appeared. "Poor Belle," he said. He put his arm around her shoulder. "It's a shame about your father."

"You know he's not crazy, Gaston!" Belle cried, hoping he might be able to talk some sense into the other villagers.

"Hmm," Gaston said. "I might be able to clear up this little misunderstanding, if . . ."

"If what?" Belle prompted.

Gaston smiled slyly. "If you marry me."

"What?" Belle could hardly believe her ears. Now she was sure that Gaston was behind this. He had convinced the townspeople that Maurice was crazy—just to try to force Belle into marrying him!

"One little word, Belle," he urged. "That's all it takes."

"Never!" Belle exclaimed furiously, pushing him away in disgust.

Gaston scowled. "Have it your way," he said, walking away haughtily. He thought he was Belle's only hope. But he was wrong.

Belle ran back inside and grabbed the magic mirror.

"My father's not crazy, and I can prove it!" she cried to the onlookers. She held up the mirror. "Show me the Beast!" she ordered it.

The mirror glowed and changed. Suddenly, the Beast appeared for everyone to see. He was howling out his misery at losing Belle, and with her, all hope for happiness. While Belle could recognize his roaring as a cry of pain and sadness, the villagers were terrified.

"Is he dangerous?" someone cried out nervously.

"Oh, no, he'd never hurt anyone," Belle assured the crowd. "I know he looks vicious, but he's really kind and gentle. He's my friend."

Gaston scowled. "If I didn't know better, I'd think you had feelings for this monster," he said accusingly.

Belle was still furious about what Gaston had tried to do. "He's no monster, Gaston," she snapped. "*You* are!"

Gaston flew into a furious rage. "She's as crazy as the old man!" he sneered, grabbing the mirror from Belle. Then he whipped the townspeople into a frenzy of fear, telling them that the Beast would steal their children in the night and destroy the village if they didn't do something about him immediately.

"We're not safe until his head is mounted on

my wall!" Gaston declared. "I say we kill the Beast!"

The crowd let out a cheer. Belle tried to stop Gaston, but it was no use. He grabbed her by the arm.

"If you're not with us, you're against us!" he shouted. He ordered the crowd to lock Belle and her father in the basement of their house so they couldn't warn the Beast that the angry mob was coming.

Belle pounded helplessly against the basement door as she heard Gaston and his followers march off toward the castle.

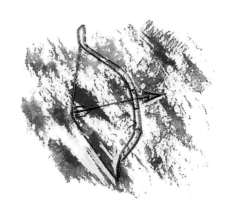

THE ATTACK

Belle was frantic. She pried at a window with a stick, but it wouldn't budge. This was all her fault!

"I have to warn the Beast!" she cried. "Oh, Papa, what are we going to do?"

"Now, now," Maurice tried to comfort her. "We'll think of something."

Luckily, little Chip was still upstairs. He went outside and peered at them through the window. He glanced nervously at the villagers marching away into the woods. As he watched them leaving, he noticed Maurice's woodchopping invention standing in the yard.

Suddenly, Chip had an idea. He managed to get the contraption moving! "Here we go!" he cried.

The ax at one end chopped at the air as it rolled down the hill toward the house. A moment later, it chopped right through the basement door, freeing Belle and Maurice!

Belle thanked Chip. Maybe now they had a chance to help save the Beast!

She and Maurice hurried outside, leaped onto Phillipe, and galloped off to the forest. Belle's heart pounded along with the horse's hooves. She had to warn the Beast! She knew that Gaston would stop at nothing in pursuit of his prey.

They rode through the darkened woods as fast as the horse could run. Would they get there in time? Belle urged Phillipe on.

Finally, the towers of the castle came into view. They rode through the gates and Maurice slipped off Phillipe's back. But Belle stayed in the saddle, staring up in horror. She had just seen the Beast, lying limply on one of the highest archways of the castle. Gaston was standing over him, a club held high over the Beast's head!

"No!" she cried.

The Beast heard her and stirred. When Belle had departed, he had been sure he would never see her again. Life hadn't seemed worth living. So when Gaston and his invaders had attacked, the Beast hadn't resisted.

But now everything had changed. She had come back!

"Belle!" the Beast murmured in wonder, hardly daring to believe she was really there. But as he lifted his head, he saw her in the courtyard below.

"No, Gaston!" she called desperately.

But Gaston paid no attention. He swung the club viciously, planning to end the Beast's life with a single blow.

But a strong arm shot upward, stopping the swing before it connected. The Beast suddenly had a reason to defend himself!

He leaped at Gaston with a loud roar. Gaston's face showed a flash of fear for the first time in his life. Then the fight was on!

Belle raced into the castle. She had to stop the two before they killed each other! She reached a balcony just above the fierce battle. She saw that the Beast had grabbed his rival by the throat and lifted him so that his feet dangled helplessly over the edge of a deadly drop-off.

Belle froze, unable to say a word. She watched as the Beast slowly pulled Gaston back to safety and dropped him on the ground.

"Get out," the Beast growled at Gaston.

"Beast!" Belle called to him with relief.

"Belle?" The Beast turned, his face lighting up with joy and wonder. He started to climb up toward her. "You came back!"

But while the Beast had shown mercy to Gaston, Gaston wasn't about to return the favor. He leaped up, pulled out a knife, and stabbed the Beast in the back!

The Beast fell back, and hung from the balcony railing. He howled in pain. But Gaston didn't have long to enjoy his victory. He lost his balance and fell, tumbling over the same drop-off the Beast had spared him from a moment earlier.

Meanwhile, Belle was hanging on to the Beast in desperation. With her help, he managed to climb up over the edge of the balcony, where he collapsed onto the ground.

Belle kneeled beside him, horrified. No! After all that had happened, the Beast couldn't die now!

The Beast opened his eyes. They were clouded with pain, but still his expression was happy as he gazed up at Belle. "You—you came back," he said again, gasping.

"Of course I came back," she replied, trying not to let her concern be heard in her voice. But it was no use. "I couldn't let them—" She broke down and

embraced him, her tears mingling with the rain that was falling. "Oh, this is all my fault. If only I'd gotten here sooner. . . ."

"Maybe it's better this way," the Beast managed to whisper.

"Don't talk like that!" Belle ordered him, her voice wavering. "You'll be all right. We're together now. Everything's going to be fine. You'll see."

She smiled weakly, trying to make herself believe it, too. The Beast smiled in return. It was a struggle to keep his eyes open, but still he gazed up at her. "At least," he said, gasping with enormous effort, "I got to see you—one last time."

With that, his eyes fell shut at last. "No!" Belle cried, feeling her heart break as his enormous body went limp. "No, please! Please don't leave me!"

She buried her face in his chest, sobbing as if she would never stop. How would she go on without him? She had just realized how important he really was to her.

"I love you," she whispered as she hugged his still body.

A MAGICAL MOMENT

For a moment, Belle continued to sob over the Beast's body. She couldn't believe he was gone. It just wasn't fair. She had finally found true love, only to have it taken away from her. It was almost as if Gaston had won, after all.

Then, suddenly, a blinding flash of light whizzed past Belle, landing on the balcony.

Belle glanced up, confused, as another flash appeared, and another, and another until she and the Beast were surrounded by a glowing, sparkling light. She stared around in amazement.

The Beast's body started to move, floating upward as if lifted by invisible hands. Belle jumped
back, startled. What was going on?

The Beast hung suspended in midair for a
moment. Suddenly, Belle realized that he was
changing in front of her eyes! His clawed hands
transformed into smooth, pale human hands. His
fangs turned into teeth. His fur became skin. He
was changing from a beast into a man!

Belle was dumbfounded. What was happening?
Where had her beloved Beast gone, and who was
this handsome young man lying before her? She
didn't understand.

Then the young man sat up
and opened his eyes. He gazed
at his transformed limbs in
disbelief that soon changed to
joy. Then he spun around
and hurried toward her.

"Belle," he said in a soft,
unfamiliar voice. "It's me!"

Belle gazed at him. Could it be? The voice, the face, the hair—it was all different. He looked nothing like the Beast.

But then she peered deeply into the young man's eyes. Yes, the eyes were familiar. They were the same eyes that had looked at her a few moments before with such tenderness and love! They wore the same expression now.

And with that, she dared to believe that what had happened was true. This *was* the Beast— changed back to his true human form.

"It *is* you!" she cried with joy. Her words of love had finally broken the spell!

Belle caressed his cheek, and he brushed the hair back from her forehead. Then he leaned down, and they shared their first kiss as more swirls of magical light surrounded

them, transforming the castle and all its servants back into their original forms.

If ever there was a reason to celebrate, this was it! Before long, Belle and her true love were dressed in their finery once again, dancing in the ballroom, surrounded by the happy servants of the castle. Maurice was there, too, thrilled to see his daughter so happy.

Belle was overjoyed as well. She had always dreamed of adventure and romance, and she had found both, more than she had ever imagined. And she had learned what the old gypsy woman had meant, too. She had learned to open up her heart. That was how she had seen the inner beauty beneath the Beast's hideous exterior, and grown to love him for who he was *inside*.

And now she would have a lifetime filled with joy to share with him. It was just like the happy ending in one of her books, only better—because this time it was real.

THE STORY OF POCAHONTAS

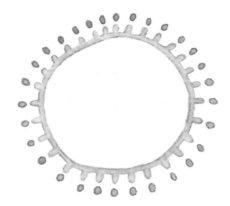

STRANGE CLOUDS

Pocahontas, the only daughter of Chief Powhatan, liked to go wherever the wind took her. With her constant companions, Meeko the raccoon and Flit the hummingbird, she explored the forests and rivers near her village.

One day, her father returned from an important battle, and wanted to find his daughter. But no one knew where she was.

Pocahontas's best friend, Nakoma, went searching for her. As she paddled her canoe down the Chicahominy River, she finally spotted Pocahontas standing on a high cliff, looking out over the river.

When Nakoma called out the news of Powhatan's return, Pocahontas smiled. Without hesitation, she dove down, down, down into the clear waters of the river. When she emerged from the water, she tipped her friend's canoe, dumping Nakoma into the river.

"Don't you think we're getting a little old for these games?" Nakoma sputtered.

In response, Pocahontas squirted a stream of water in her friend's face. Nakoma shrieked with

laughter and splashed her. Soon the two of them were having a water fight.

When they had tired of the game, the two friends righted Nakoma's canoe and climbed in. "What were you doing up there?" Nakoma asked.

"Thinking," Pocahontas replied as she squeezed water from her long, thick, dark hair.

"About the dream again?" Nakoma knew about the dream her friend had been having lately. Something to do with a spinning arrow . . .

But there was no time to think about that now. The two girls paddled quickly back to the village, where Powhatan was talking about the battle his warriors had just won.

"Our warriors fought with courage," he was saying as Pocahontas and Nakoma joined the crowd, "but none as bravely as Kocoum." He gestured to a stern young warrior standing beside him.

"Oh, he is so handsome," Nakoma whispered, watching as the tribe's medicine man painted Kocoum's broad chest with symbols of his bravery.

Pocahontas smirked. "I especially love his smile," she said. She respected Kocoum's strength as a warrior. But why did he always have to look so serious?

When the chief finished his speech, Pocahontas hurried to greet him. "My daughter!" Powhatan said when he saw her, reaching out for a hug. "Seeing you gives me great joy. Come with me. We have much to talk about."

Pocahontas walked with her father into a nearby longhouse. She was eager to tell him about her dream. He was so wise—perhaps he would be able to tell her what it meant.

"Father, for many nights now I've been having a

very strange dream," she said. "I think it's telling me something's about to happen. Something exciting!"

"Yes," Powhatan agreed with a smile. "Something exciting *is* about to happen. Kocoum has asked to seek your hand in marriage."

Pocahontas was startled at her father's words. "Marry Kocoum?" she said. "But he's so—*serious*."

Powhatan chuckled at her surprise. "My daughter, Kocoum will make a fine husband. With him you will be safe from harm."

"Father, I think my dream is pointing me down another path," Pocahontas protested.

"This is the right path for you." Powhatan knew that his daughter was a free spirit, just as her mother had been. But even free spirits had to settle down sometime. "Even the wild mountain stream must someday join the big river," he told her gently.

Pocahontas gazed out at the river. She understood what her father was saying. But she just couldn't imagine spending the rest of her life as Kocoum's wife. It seemed too safe, too easy. Too *boring*.

Her father pulled a beautiful shell necklace out of his clothes. "Your mother wore this for our wedding," he said, fastening it around his daughter's neck. "It was her dream to see you wear it at your own."

Pocahontas was too overwhelmed and confused to say another word to her father.

Later, Pocahontas and her animal friends sat by the river's edge. "He wants me to be steady like the river," Pocahontas murmured, staring into the water as it moved smoothly past the shore. Just then, a pair of playful otters began splashing around, and Pocahontas laughed at their antics. "But it's not steady at all! It's always changing. . . ."

She decided it was time to seek advice from the one creature even wiser than her father. So Pocahontas paddled down the Chicahominy in her canoe. When she reached a fork in the great river, she didn't go down the broad, smooth-flowing waters to the left. Instead, she turned down the right-hand fork, which twisted and turned over rocks and rapids as it flowed through a deep forest.

Soon Pocahontas was pulling her canoe into a

glade. There, a wise old spirit lived within a four-hundred-year-old willow tree. Her name was Grandmother Willow, and she had been like a mother to Pocahontas since the girl's own mother had died many years earlier.

As Pocahontas's canoe glided into the glade, the bark of the ancient willow's trunk formed into a kindly, wrinkled, smiling face. "Is that my Pocahontas?" Grandmother Willow 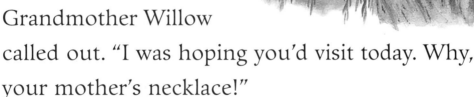 called out. "I was hoping you'd visit today. Why, your mother's necklace!"

"That's what I wanted to talk to you about." Pocahontas touched the necklace. "My father wants me to marry Kocoum."

"Kocoum?" Grandmother Willow said. She sounded surprised and slightly dismayed. "But he's so serious!"

"I know," Pocahontas agreed. "My father thinks

it's the right path for me. But lately I've been having this dream, and—"

"Oh, a dream!" Grandmother Willow exclaimed. "Let's hear all about it."

Pocahontas quickly described her dream. "I'm running through the woods," she said. "And then, right there in front of me is an arrow. As I look at it, it starts to spin—faster and faster and faster until suddenly it stops."

"Hmm." Grandmother Willow looked thoughtful. "It seems to me, this spinning arrow is pointing you down your path."

"But what is my path?" Pocahontas asked. "How am I ever going to find it?"

Grandmother Willow chuckled. "Your mother asked me the very same question."

"She did?" Pocahontas was surprised. "What did you tell her?"

"I told her to listen," Grandmother Willow replied. "All around you are spirits, child. If you listen, they will guide you."

Pocahontas did her best to do as Grandmother Willow said. She listened, opening herself up to any messages she might find in the earth, the trees, the water, the sky.

"I hear the wind," she said in wonder.

"Yes," Grandmother Willow said. "What is it telling you?"

"I don't understand. . . ." Pocahontas did her best to listen even closer to the breeze rustling the treetops. What was it saying?

"What does your heart hear?" Grandmother
Willow asked.

Pocahontas closed her eyes and reached out with
her heart, trying to hear the message she knew was
out there. Suddenly, she understood the voice of the
wind.

"It says something's coming—strange clouds?"
she said.

She wasn't sure what that meant. But something
told her to climb up into Grandmother Willow's top

branches. From there, she had a view over the tree-tops, all the way to the waters of the bay.

To her amazement, she saw billowing white shapes that looked like clouds floating over the ocean. Pocahontas couldn't take her eyes off the white shapes as they fluttered and danced in the breeze.

"Clouds," she murmured. She didn't know exactly what she was seeing, but a shudder ran through her. Yes, something was coming, just as her dream had predicted . . . something new and exciting—"strange clouds."

LISTEN TO NATURE

In the harbor, a group of adventurers from England surveyed the new land that lay before them. One of the sailors, a tall, handsome man named John Smith, led the way off the ship.

"Come on, men," he said cheerfully. "We didn't come all this way just to look at it."

Soon the men were busy tying the ship in its new port and unloading supplies. But John Smith wanted to get a closer look at the wilderness right away.

Meanwhile, Pocahontas had crept as close to the harbor as she dared. From her favorite overlook, she

watched as the tall man broke away from the group. In some ways he looked much like the men of her village. But he had unusual light-colored hair, and his clothes looked very peculiar to her.

Who was this stranger? What was he doing here? Pocahontas shrank back into the forest as the man climbed up the rocks, almost to the overlook. He surveyed the landscape with interest, but he didn't spot Pocahontas in her hiding place.

Meeko, curious like all raccoons, couldn't resist the temptation to get a closer look at the newcomer. With  an eager laugh, he scurried out toward the end of the overlook. Pocahontas tried to stop him, but he wriggled free.

The little raccoon leaped across to the tree where the man stood. He bumped into the man's boots.

John Smith was startled by the sudden thump against his legs. "Hey!" he cried, automatically drawing his knife.

He looked around, but didn't see an enemy anywhere. Finally, he looked down and spotted the raccoon at his feet. His face relaxed into a smile.

"Well!" he exclaimed. "You're a strange-looking fellow. Are you hungry?"

He pulled a few biscuits from his bag. Meeko sniffed at one suspiciously, then grabbed it and chewed it happily.

John Smith laughed. "You like it, eh?"

Pocahontas smiled as she watched. She didn't

understand the words this stranger spoke, but there was something about his face that she liked. She watched until a shout rose from below, calling the man back to his ship. Then she carefully and silently made her way back into the woods.

Meanwhile, at the village, the tribe was already discussing the newcomers. Kekata, the medicine man, had consulted the spirits, which had said that the strangers had weapons that spouted fire and would consume everything in their path. Worried about this new threat to his people, Powhatan had sent Kocoum with a scouting party to observe and find out more about the strangers.

Pocahontas was still watching the newcomers herself. She had made her way down through the woods closer to the beach. There, she had a clear view of the activity as the men planted a flag, unloaded more supplies, and began to set up a camp. The strange white shapes she saw approaching from the top of Grandmother Willow's tree were attached to these newcomers' ships!

Seconds later, she noticed the tall blond man glancing at the forest. He seemed very distracted from the work he was doing. Finally, he moved away from the others and entered the woods, clutching a long, thin stick-like object in his hands.

Pocahontas followed him, moving like a shadow from tree to tree. She could tell that the man was excited about the unfamiliar landscape around him. He climbed over rocks, swung from vines, and surveyed the tallest treetops.

Pocahontas smiled as she tracked him from cliff to valley to forest. He truly seemed to appreciate her beautiful home.

Finally, John Smith came upon a magnificent waterfall emptying into a clear river. He bent to splash his face with the cool, refreshing water. As he cupped water into his hands, he caught the reflection of movement in it. What was that? Something —or some*one*—was hiding in the trees on a rise behind him.

Instantly on guard, he glanced over his shoulder without moving his head. Who was there? Could it be one of the savages they'd expected to find in this wild land?

Pocahontas lost sight of the stranger as he moved away from the river's edge. She crept carefully down the rise, looking around. Where had he gone?

She stepped out onto the rocky shore, wondering how he had disappeared so suddenly. She had only taken her eyes off him for a moment. . . .

Meanwhile, John Smith was hiding behind the waterfall with his musket at the ready. He wasn't about to let a savage take him by surprise! By now he could see that the figure on the other side of the sheet of falling water was human, though he couldn't tell much beyond that.

When the figure stepped across to a rock just in front of where he was hiding, John Smith jumped out and aimed his musket. But he stopped short before firing, his jaw dropping in surprise. It was a woman—a beautiful young woman dressed in a deerskin garment, with flowing dark hair and deep black eyes!

Pocahontas stared at the stranger. A small part of her mind was ashamed for allowing herself to be seen. But most of her attention was focused on the man.

He was tall, as tall as the tallest warriors of her tribe. His eyes were blue, like the brightest ocean water. And what was that strange

staff he was holding, pointing at her?

She wondered if it held magic, like the staff Kekata used at certain tribal ceremonies.

The two stared at each other in silence. After a moment, the man lowered his staff to the ground and stepped toward Pocahontas. She held her ground for a moment, watching him come closer.

Then, all of a sudden, she realized where she was. What was she thinking? She knew nothing about this stranger. For all she knew he could be a ghost or an evil spirit come to carry her off. Turning quickly, she raced toward the safety of the forest.

"No, wait!" John Smith called after her. He chased Pocahontas through the woods to another part of the river.

Pocahontas leaped into a wooden canoe she knew was docked there. As she prepared to push off from shore, John Smith skidded to a stop. He held out his hands to show he meant no harm.

"Please," he called. "Don't run off. I'm not going to hurt you."

He took a few careful steps forward. She gazed at him suspiciously, but didn't move.

He stretched out his hand. "Let me help you out of there."

She said a few words in a language he didn't recognize.

"You don't understand a word I'm saying, do you?" John Smith asked. Still, he held out his hand, palm up, hoping his body language would express his good intentions. As soon as he'd seen this beautiful young woman, he had wanted to know more about her.

Pocahontas stared at the fair stranger for a moment. His words were strange, but his meaning was clear. He wanted to help her from her canoe. Should she accept his offered hand? She had no reason to trust him, but something in his eyes made her stretch out her own hand.

As soon as their hands touched, the wind began to sing and swirl around them. Pocahontas heard a distant voice—Grandmother Willow's voice. *What does your heart hear?* she crooned.

Pocahontas's eyes widened. She stepped out onto the shore, still holding the stranger's hand. They looked into each other's eyes. The man spoke to her again, his words still sounding unfamiliar.

She closed her eyes, waiting for the wind to speak to her. Suddenly, she heard its message sweeping through her heart. The stranger was asking her a question: *Who are you?*

Opening her eyes, she answered him. "Pocahontas," she said simply.

"What?" John Smith was surprised to hear the young woman speak. "What did you say?"

"My name is Pocahontas."

John Smith was amazed. He had understood her! He wasn't sure how it had happened, but it was wonderful. "I'm John Smith," he said with a smile.

NATIVES

Pocahontas stared at the strange object on John Smith's head. It was made of a smooth and shiny material she didn't recognize.

"It's called a helmet," John told her.

"Helmet," Pocahontas repeated softly, savoring the sound of the new word.

The two of them were sitting on a grassy bluff overlooking the river. For the past few minutes, they had been getting to know each other. John had learned that Pocahontas was a daughter of the powerful tribe of Powhatan, whose people had lived on this land for many generations. In turn, John had shared some of his own background. He had explained that he and his shipmates had come from a far-off land across the sea, and that he loved to explore new lands. What he didn't tell her was that the leader of the expedition, Governor Ratcliffe, had already claimed the new land for the king of England, or that he planned to chase out any Indians he found while digging up the forest in search of gold. What would she say if she knew all that?

Not wanting to think about that anymore, he cleared his throat and looked out over the water. "So, what river is this?" he asked.

"Quiyoughcohannock," Pocahontas replied.

"You have the most unusual names here!" John said in amazement. "Chicahominy. Qui—Qui-yough-co-hannock. Pocahontas."

Pocahontas smiled shyly as he looked at her. "You have the most unusual name, too," she said. "John Smith."

At that moment, John noticed a little striped tail poking out of his bag. "Hey!" he cried, pulling out the same mischievous raccoon he had seen on the ridge over the harbor. "Is this bottomless pit a friend of yours?" he asked Pocahontas.

"Meeko!" Pocahontas chided, picking up the little raccoon.

"Well, how do you do, Meeko?" John offered his hand to the little creature.

Meeko grabbed it and peered at it, clearly hoping for some more biscuits.

Meanwhile, Pocahontas stared curiously at John's outstretched palm. Noticing her curious expression, he smiled.

"It's just a handshake," he explained. "Here, let me show you." He took Pocahontas's hand in his own and shook it up and down. "It's how we say hello."

"This is how we say hello," Pocahontas said. She raised one hand, palm facing forward, and traced a circle in the air. "*Win-gap-o*," she said in her own language.

"Wing-gap-o," John repeated, carefully copying word and motion.

"And how we say good-bye," Pocahontas went on, beginning to trace a circle in the opposite direction.

John Smith smiled and caught her palm with his own in midcircle. "I like 'hello' better," he said.

They stood smiling at each other for a moment, their hands resting against each other. They were interrupted by Meeko, who had just grabbed something else out of John's bag and raced off with it. This time it wasn't a biscuit, but a small, round item.

"What was that?" Pocahontas asked.

"My compass," John said. "It tells you how to find your way when you get lost. But it's all right—I'll get another one in London."

"London? Is that your village?" Pocahontas asked curiously.

"Yes, it's a very big village," he replied. "It's got streets filled with carriages, bridges over the rivers, and buildings as tall as trees."

Pocahontas couldn't imagine it. "I'd like to see those things!" she exclaimed.

"You will," John replied. "We're going to build them here. We'll show your people how to use this land properly." Now that he had come to know Pocahontas, he realized there was no need to chase her tribe off the land. He was sure these Indians would be able to live in peace with the new settlers. "We'll build roads and decent houses, and—"

Somehow, Pocahontas didn't seem excited about

the plans. "Our houses are fine," she interrupted.

"You think that," he assured her, "only because you don't know any better. We've improved the lives of savages all over the world!"

"Savages!" Pocahontas cried.

John tried to explain, but Pocahontas was angry with him now. How dare he come here, to her home, and insult her?

Still, she couldn't help wanting to help him understand. Just because her people were different from his, he thought that meant they were less civilized. She would just have to show him that wasn't true.

Taking him by the hand, she led him into the forest. If her own words were not enough to convince him, perhaps the spirits of nature, the voices of the wind and trees and water, could help her explain his error.

Mingling her voice with the songs of the earth, Pocahontas showed John a world he'd never realized was there—right in front of his eyes. She introduced him to the spirits that lived within everything, from an

ordinary boulder to the noble eagles soaring overhead.

He looked into the eyes of shy forest creatures—deer, otters, a playful bear cub—and
saw them look back at him. He leaped head-
first from a waterfall, becoming part of its flow before
splashing into the water below. He ran with Pocahontas
down the hidden trails of the deepest pine forest and
tasted wild berries warmed by the sun. As the sun set, he
gazed up at the patterns of the stars overhead with new
eyes.

For the first time, he began to understand that everything around him was a part of the intricate pattern of life
on earth, from the vibrant young woman standing beside
him to the copper-colored leaves blowing in the wind.
Every living thing had its own spirit, from the tiniest
sapling to the ancient sycamore towering overhead.

On that magical afternoon, lost in the eyes of a young
woman who, just a short time before, would have seemed
to him a savage, John Smith felt his heart beating to a
new rhythm. He was finally learning to recognize the
voices of the natural world all around him.

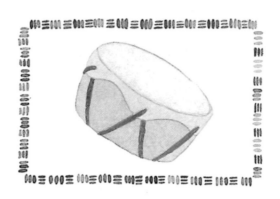

DRUMS OF WAR

Pocahontas was hardly aware of time passing as she and John Smith explored the forest together. But suddenly, she heard a distant, threatening sound through the trees.

"The drums," she said anxiously. "They mean trouble. I shouldn't be here."

John didn't understand. Why did she look so distressed all of a sudden? "I want to see you again," he said.

"I'm sorry. I have to go," Pocahontas murmured, racing off without a backward glance.

She ran home as fast as she could, worrying all the way about the drums—the drums of war. What did they mean?

When she reached the village, Nakoma told her everything. The chief had sent a party to spy on the strangers, but the spies had been seen. The pale men had attacked the warriors with strange sticks that spouted flames, and one of the tribe's finest warriors, Namontack, had been gravely injured.

That wasn't all. Before the attack, the warriors had seen that the newcomers were building a fort, cutting down trees, and digging huge holes in the earth.

Pocahontas was dismayed. Was this the help John Smith had spoken of? Did his people think they would help her people by wounding their warriors and cutting down trees?

Powhatan found his daughter and Nakoma gathering corn. "You should be inside the village," he told them.

"We're gathering food for when the warriors arrive," Nakoma explained. She had already told Pocahontas that Powhatan had called upon all the warriors of his allies' tribes to come to help them fight this new threat.

Powhatan nodded. "Don't go far," he warned. "Now is not the time to be running off."

"Yes, Father," Pocahontas agreed, though she couldn't help thinking of John Smith. Where was he now—with his own tribesmen, helping to dig up the earth?

"When I see you wear that necklace," Powhatan said gently, his grim expression softening, "you look just like your mother."

"I miss her," Pocahontas murmured, touching the shell pendant at her throat. If only her mother

were still alive—maybe she could advise Pocahontas what to do about her confusing feelings. Maybe she would understand her daughter's fascination with the strange man from over the sea.

"But she is still with us," Powhatan said with a smile. "Whenever the wind blows through the trees, I feel her presence. Our people looked to her for wisdom and strength. Someday they will look to you as well."

"I would be honored by that," Pocahontas said.

"You shouldn't be out here alone," the chief said to the two young women. "I will send Kocoum."

Pocahontas sighed as her father left. She had never felt so confused. It was as if she were being pulled in two different directions—toward the tribe she'd always honored and loved, and also toward the unusual new man who had captured her heart. She didn't know what she really wanted. But she certainly didn't feel like seeing Kocoum just then.

"All right, what is it?" Nakoma interrupted her thoughts. "You're hiding something." She had known Pocahontas a long time. She could tell something was troubling her deeply.

"I'm not hiding anything," Pocahontas insisted. Though she had shared many secrets with Nakoma, she couldn't tell her the truth this time. It would only get Nakoma in trouble.

Just then, the cornstalks rustled behind them. Nakoma gasped as John Smith stepped out. "Pocahontas, look!" she cried, her voice filled with fear. "It's one of them, I am going to get—"

Pocahontas clapped her hand over her friend's mouth. She stared at John. "What are you doing here?"

"I had to see you again," John replied.

"Pocahontas! Pocahontas?"

Pocahontas gulped. Kocoum was calling her from somewhere nearby. She had to get John out of there before the warrior saw him. "Please, don't say anything," she begged Nakoma quietly. Then she grabbed John's hand. "Quick, this way!"

She pulled him into the cornstalks seconds before Kocoum appeared.

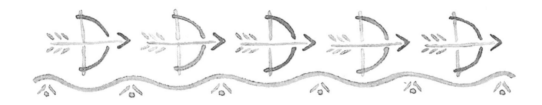

THE COLOR OF GOLD

"This place is incredible," John said as Pocahontas led him across a natural bridge into the enchanted glade. Meeko and Flit came along, though Flit didn't seem happy that Pocahontas was bringing a stranger to this special place. The little hummingbird flew in and out of John's path, making it difficult for him to keep up. "And to think, we came all this way just to dig it up for gold."

"Gold?" Pocahontas said, not recognizing the word. "What's gold?"

"You know, it's yellow, comes out of the ground, it's really valuable," John replied.

"Oh!" Pocahontas reached into her bag. She pulled out one of the ears of golden corn she and Nakoma had been picking. "Here, we have lots of it. Gold."

John laughed and shook his head. "No, gold is . . . this," he said, pulling a coin out of his pocket.

"Hmm," Pocahontas said, examining the coin. "There's nothing like that around here."

Meeko grabbed the coin from her hand and nibbled it eagerly. When he realized it wasn't good to eat, he tossed it away in disgust.

John shook his head in dismay. "All this way for nothing," he said. "Well, those boys are in for a big surprise." He could imagine the look on Governor Ratcliffe's face when he heard the news. Ratcliffe was counting on this trip to make his fortune. Now it seemed there was no fortune to be found here.

"Will they leave?" Pocahontas asked. But what she really wanted to know was whether John would be leaving.

"Some of them might," he replied, lying back and staring up at the tree branches overhead.

Pocahontas had to ask the question in her heart. "Will you go home?"

John sat up. "Well, it's not like I have much of a home to go back to. I've never really belonged anywhere."

"You could belong here," Pocahontas said softly.

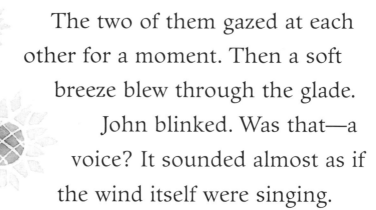

The two of them gazed at each other for a moment. Then a soft breeze blew through the glade. John blinked. Was that—a voice? It sounded almost as if the wind itself were singing.

Suddenly, the old willow trunk in front of him shifted and formed an ancient-looking face. John stared, hardly believing his own eyes.

"What was that?" he exclaimed.

"Hello, John Smith." Grandmother Willow greeted him with a smile.

John gulped. "Pocahontas," he said, "that tree is talking to me."

"Then you should talk back," Pocahontas whispered.

"Don't be frightened, young man," Grandmother Willow said. "My bark is worse than my bite."

"Say something," Pocahontas urged John.

John looked uncomfortable. "What do you say to a tree?"

"Come closer, John Smith," Grandmother Willow said. John stepped forward, and soon the ancient tree spirit was staring directly into his eyes. "He has a good soul," she said after a moment. "And he's handsome, too!"

"Oh, I like her," John said with a chuckle.

Pocahontas laughed. "I knew you would."

"Smith! Smith, where are you, mate?"

The smile disappeared from John's face. He recognized the voices of his shipmates, Ben and Lon. "We can't let them see us," he whispered to Pocahontas, pulling her out of sight behind Grandmother Willow's thick trunk. "I'd better get back before they send the whole camp out after me."

"When will I see you again?" Pocahontas asked.

John turned and touched her cheek gently. "Meet me tonight," he said. "Right here."

After one last long look, he turned away and hurried back toward camp.

Pocahontas was left alone with Grandmother Willow. "What am I doing?" Pocahontas exclaimed, pacing back and forth. "I shouldn't be seeing him again. I mean, I *want* to see him again—something inside is telling me it's the right thing."

"Perhaps it's your dream," Grandmother Willow suggested.

"My dream," Pocahontas repeated thoughtfully. "Do you think he's the one the spinning arrow was pointing to?"

It was a new thought, and an interesting one. Pocahontas only wished she knew what it all meant.

RIPPLES IN THE WATER

As Pocahontas returned to the village a few minutes later, she saw a great number of warriors gathered on the shore of the river. More were arriving in canoes—her father's allies in other tribes had sent their warriors to help fight the new invaders.

Nakoma spotted Pocahontas. She looked terribly worried. "Pocahontas, are you crazy?" she cried. "What were you doing with—"

Before she could finish the sentence, Kocoum strode up to them. "There you are," he interrupted, sounding less stern than usual. "Look at them!" He put a hand on Pocahontas's shoulder and turned her toward the crowd of warriors. "Now we have enough warriors to destroy those white demons!"

Pocahontas could hear the excitement in Kocoum's voice. She guessed that he was looking forward to the coming battle. Her heart sank. How could she ever convince her people to talk of peace when they were already preparing for war?

She thought of John. For him, she had to try.

Spotting her father standing with the chief of one of the allied tribes, she hurried over to him. "Father, I need to speak with you."

"Not now, my daughter," Powhatan replied. "The council is gathering."

"We don't have to fight them!" Pocahontas cried as he turned away. "There must be a better way."

The chief turned back, his face solemn. "Sometimes our paths are chosen for us."

"But maybe we should try talking to them," Pocahontas suggested.

"They do not want to talk," he answered.

"But if one of them did want to talk?" Pocahontas asked desperately. "You would listen to him, wouldn't you?"

Powhatan sighed deeply. "Of course I would," he said. "But it is not that simple. Nothing is simple anymore."

Pocahontas watched as her father turned away and joined the council. Her father's words had given her a slight hope. She knew a man who would want to talk—to make peace with the tribe. When she met John that evening at the enchanted glade, the two of them would have to figure out a plan.

A little while later, as Pocahontas hurried away from the village through the cornfields, she heard a voice call out to her. She spun around. "Nakoma!" Pocahontas cried.

"Don't go out there," Nakoma warned. "I lied for you once. Don't ask me to do it again!"

Pocahontas turned away. "I have to do this."

"He's one of them!" Nakoma grabbed her friend by the arm.

"You don't know him," Pocahontas replied.

"If you go out there, you'll be turning your back on your own people," Nakoma said.

"I'm trying to help my people!" Pocahontas cried.

"Pocahontas, you're my best friend," Nakoma pleaded. "I don't want you to get hurt."

Pocahontas could tell that her friend was truly worried. But she could feel the time slipping away. She had to find John as soon as possible—everything depended on it! Nakoma would just have to trust her.

"I know what I'm doing," Pocahontas said, pulling away. She ignored Nakoma's cries as she ran into the tall forest of corn.

When Pocahontas reached the glade a few minutes later, Grandmother Willow was awaiting her anxiously. "The earth is trembling, child. What's happened?"

"The warriors are here," Pocahontas replied. There was no time to explain further, because suddenly John was standing beside her.

"Pocahontas," he said, his voice filled with worry. He grasped her hands in his own. "Listen to me. My men are planning to attack your people—you've got to warn them."

"Maybe it's not too late to stop this," Pocahontas said. "You have to come with me and talk to my father."

She began to drag him toward the village. But John held her back. "Pocahontas, talking isn't going to do any good," he said grimly. "I already tried talking to my men. But everything about this land has them spooked." He shrugged. "Once two sides want to fight, nothing can stop them."

"Now then, there's something I want to show you." Grandmother Willow's voice interrupted the tense moment. She lowered a long, slender branch toward the still water below. "Look."

The end of the branch touched the surface of the water, forming a ripple. The small circle of motion spread outward, becoming larger and larger.

"The ripples," Pocahontas said, seeing her point right away.

But John didn't understand so quickly. "What about them?" he asked.

"So small at first!" Grandmother Willow said. "Then look how they grow. But someone has to start them."

Finally, John understood what the ancient spirit was saying. But he didn't think it would work. "They're not going to listen to us," he said.

"Young man," Grandmother Willow chided, "sometimes the right path is not the easiest one. Don't you see? Only when the fighting stops can you be together."

On that point, John couldn't argue. He gazed down at Pocahontas, taking her hands in his own once again. He had to try—for her. Even if it

seemed hopeless, he and
Pocahontas had to try.

"All right," he said.
"Let's go talk to
your father."

Pocahontas was
overcome with
hope. With John
beside her, she could
help change her father's mind—she knew she could!
She flung her arms around him.

He hugged her back, then pulled away. They
stared into each other's eyes. Then their lips met,
and for a long moment everything else, even the
coming battle, faded away.

All of a sudden, a bloodcurdling war cry made
them jump. It was Kocoum! The warrior, filled with
rage, flung himself upon John.

"Kocoum! No!" Pocahontas cried as the two men struggled. "Stop!"

But before she could do anything, a shot echoed through the forest.

THE PRISONER

Kocoum grimaced in pain and toppled backward. He reached out to catch himself, but his hand locked onto Pocahontas's shell necklace. As he fell to the ground, the necklace came apart and broke into tiny pieces.

Pocahontas couldn't believe this was happening. But who had shot Kocoum? John was unarmed.

"Thomas!" John Smith cried as a frightened-looking young man ran out of the forest, clutching one of the pale men's strange war sticks.

Pocahontas fell to her knees at Kocoum's side. His

eyes were closed and his body was still. "You killed him!" she accused, glaring up at the newcomer.

Just then, the sound of many voices echoed through the forest. The Indian warriors were coming.

John gestured at Thomas. "Get out of here," he ordered, knowing that the young man was in grave danger.

Thomas hesitated, still looking terrified. He had thought he was protecting John against the Indians—

how could he have known it would cause so much trouble? Turning, he raced off into the forest.

Seconds later, the warriors arrived. They grabbed John and bound his arms behind him as Pocahontas watched helplessly, overwhelmed with guilt, confusion, and grief.

Back at the village, the moonlight outlined the faces of the Indians gathered around Kocoum's body. Powhatan's eyes were sad and grim.

"Who did this?" he demanded.

The warriors were dragging John toward the chief. "Pocahontas was out in the woods," one of the men said. "Kocoum went to find her, and this white man attacked him."

Powhatan approached John, who had been pushed to his knees in the clearing. "Your weapons are strong," the chief told the stranger. "But now our anger is stronger." He turned away to address his people. "At sunrise, he will be the first to die!"

Pocahontas stepped forward. She had to explain what had really happened. It was as much her own fault as it was John's! "But, father—" she began.

"I told you to stay in the village!" Powhatan interrupted, his eyes cold as he looked at her. "You disobeyed me. You have shamed your father."

"I was only trying to help," Pocahontas protested.

Her father would not listen. "Because of your foolishness, Kocoum is dead," he said.

Pocahontas sank to her knees as her father ordered the warriors to take John away. She stared at the ground, feeling hopeless. How had everything gone so terribly wrong?

A shadow fell across the ground. Looking up, she saw Nakoma standing before her.

"Kocoum was just coming to protect me," Pocahontas told her friend sadly.

"Pocahontas," Nakoma said, her voice choked with grief. "*I* sent Kocoum after you. I was worried about you. I thought I was doing the right thing!"

Pocahontas was startled by her friend's confession. But she was not angry. Like Kocoum, Nakoma had only had her best interests at heart. How could she blame either one of them for what had happened?

"All this happened because of me," Pocahontas said. "And now I'll never see John Smith again." She felt as if her heart were breaking.

Nakoma reached for her hand. She had let Pocahontas down once—she wouldn't do it again. "Come with me," she said.

A moment later, the two of them were standing before the prison hut. The warriors guarding the entrance looked at them in surprise.

Nakoma pushed her friend forward. "Pocahontas wants to look into the eyes of the man who killed Kocoum," she said firmly.

The warriors exchanged a glance. They knew the chief's daughter had a fiery spirit. Perhaps they shouldn't have been surprised to see her here.

"Be quick," one of them said, moving aside to let Pocahontas pass.

Pocahontas entered the hut. The interior was dark except for a moonbeam shining through the smoke hole in the roof. Its light revealed John Smith, who was bound to the center pole.

"Pocahontas!" he cried when he saw her.

"I'm so sorry," she whispered, overcome with emotion. She leaned against him for strength. "It would have been better if we'd never met—none of this would have ever happened!"

"Pocahontas, look at me," John insisted. He waited until she met his gaze, then went on: "I'd rather die tomorrow than live a hundred years without knowing you."

She gazed back at him, knowing that he spoke the truth, because she felt the same way herself. Even after all the terrible things that had happened, and all that were to come, she couldn't truly wish to change the past. She couldn't imagine going back to a time when she had not known John Smith.

"Pocahontas," Nakoma called softly from the door of the hut. The warriors were becoming impatient.

Pocahontas hardly heard her. She ran her fingers over John's face, her eyes memorizing its lines.

"I can't leave you," she said quietly.

"You never will," John replied with certainty. "No matter what happens to me, I'll always be with you—forever."

His calm courage gave Pocahontas strength. With one last caress, she stood and left the hut.

THE RIGHT PATH

"They're going to kill him at sunrise, Grandmother Willow," Pocahontas said, her voice filled with pain as she sat before the ancient tree spirit.

"You have to stop them," Grandmother Willow replied.

"I can't!" Pocahontas cried. How could she stop this terrible thing from happening? She hadn't even been able to convince her own father to talk to the newcomers. And now, she had shamed her father by talking to a settler on her own.

"Child, remember your dream!" Grandmother Willow encouraged.

Her dream—that was where all this tragedy had started. "I was wrong, Grandmother Willow," Pocahontas said. "I followed the wrong path. I feel so lost."

Even Pocahontas's animal friends, Meeko and Flit, were filled with sadness. They watched as she buried her face in her hands.

But suddenly Meeko brightened. Lost? He had heard that word before.

Racing for the hollow of an old tree trunk, the little raccoon rustled around in the goodies he had stashed there. Soon he found what he was looking for.

Pocahontas looked up as Meeko nudged something at her. What was it? She picked up the round, shiny object and stared at it.

"The compass," she said, wondering why Meeko had brought it to her. She remembered when the mischievous raccoon had taken it, and she hadn't seen it since. On one side, there were marks around

the edge of the circle. And in the middle was—a spinning arrow! Pocahontas gasped in astonishment.

"It's the arrow from your dream!" Grandmother Willow exclaimed.

Suddenly, things didn't feel so hopeless after all. "I was right!" Pocahontas cried. "It *was* pointing to him!" As she stared at the compass, a beam of light broke over the horizon. "Sunrise!" she said anxiously.

"It's not too late, child," Grandmother Willow

urged. "Let the spirits of the earth guide you. You know your path, child. Now follow it!"

Pocahontas knew her wise old friend was right, as usual. Springing into a run, she raced toward the village. The leaves of the trees seemed to part for her; the wind sustained her with invisible wings as she leaped from one rock to another. Still, she wasn't sure it would be enough. The rays of the morning sun grew stronger. Would she make it back in time?

At the same moment, Governor Ratcliffe was leading his men toward the Indian village, while Powhatan's warriors brought John Smith to the stone slab on the overlook. There, the execution would take place.

As one of Powhatan's men handed the chief his war club, another pushed John's head onto the slab. It was time to avenge Kocoum's death.

Powhatan raised the club. Below, he saw the new-comers emerge from the woods. They looked up, shouting angry words. But Powhatan didn't hesitate.

He raised the war club higher in the air, preparing to bring it down on John Smith's head with a killing blow.

Suddenly, Pocahontas appeared. She saw what her father was about to do. There was no time to call out to him, no time for reasoning. "No!" she shouted. With one last burst of energy, she ran forward and flung herself onto John's body, covering his head with her own.

Powhatan stopped in midswing, startled by his daughter's action. Pocahontas stared up at him defiantly.

"If you kill him, you will have to kill me, too!" she cried.

Powhatan frowned. "Daughter, stand back!" he ordered.

"I won't!" Pocahontas shouted. "I love him, Father."

Powhatan's eyes widened in surprise. Had he heard her right? Had his only daughter just claimed to love this stranger—this murderer?

In the valley below, the Englishmen had seen what Pocahontas had done. They murmured amongst themselves, wondering what was going on.

But Pocahontas paid attention only to her father. "Look around you," Pocahontas urged the chief. "This is where the path of hatred has brought us." She wrapped her arms more tightly around John's head. "This is the path I choose, Father. What will yours be?"

Powhatan looked around him. On one side, he saw the strangers holding their fire-breathing weapons at the ready. On the other side, his own warriors stood prepared to fight to the death for the tribe.

And in front of him, his daughter, his only child,

looked up at him with eyes full of strength and
love.

At that moment, a gentle breeze blew up toward
him from the valley, blowing through the trees and
carrying their beautiful, multicolored leaves along
in a dance of joy. He closed his eyes, listening for
the spirit of his beloved wife. What was she telling
him?

Suddenly, he took his club in both hands and

raised it high above his head. "My daughter speaks with a wisdom beyond her years," he announced. "We have all come here with anger in our hearts. But she comes with courage and understanding. From this day forward, if there is to be more killing, it will not start with me." He lowered the club and glanced at his men. "Release him."

Pocahontas smiled as the Indian warriors lowered their weapons. One of the men untied John's arms. She had done it! Now John would be safe.

"Fire!" a voice cried from below. It was Governor Ratcliffe—he still wanted to attack, even though the Indians didn't want to fight.

But his men had been affected by the scene they had just witnessed. They refused to raise their weapons.

"Fine, I'll settle this myself!" Ratcliffe grabbed a musket from one of the men. Raising it to his shoulder, he took aim at the chief standing on the overlook.

John Smith had his arms around Pocahontas. Over her shoulder, he caught a glimpse of Ratcliffe below. In a split second, he realized what the cruel governor intended to do.

"No!" he cried. Leaping toward Powhatan, John Smith shoved the chief out of the bullet's path—putting himself directly in the line of fire.

Seeing what was happening, Pocahontas leaped forward herself. But this time she was too late to save John from harm. Her eyes widened in horror as she saw his body jerk from the force of the bullet.

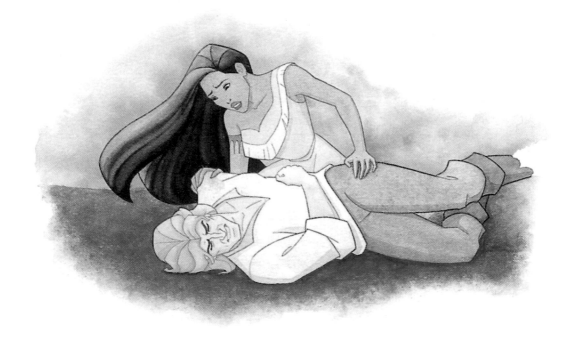

✻　✻　✻

Some time later, a pair of Englishmen were loading a dinghy with supplies to be sent out to the main ship. They looked up to see Thomas approaching. They knew he had been tending to John's wound.

"Is he going to make it, Thomas?" one of them asked.

Thomas sighed. "The sooner he gets back to England, the better." He knew that John was lucky to be alive at all. If he wanted to stay that way, he needed a doctor's care. "Is the ship ready yet?" he asked.

"Any minute now," one of the men replied.

Thomas nodded and returned to John, who was resting on a makeshift stretcher farther up the beach. "We'd better get you on board," Thomas told him.

"No, not yet," John said weakly. "She said she'd be here."

Thomas looked over his shoulder as he heard a sound from the woods. "Look!" he cried.

John lifted his head despite the pain. He saw a long line of people step out of the mist, all holding baskets of food and other supplies. At the head of the group was Pocahontas. As the others set down their gifts, she stepped forward.

Thomas spoke to Pocahontas as she passed him. "Going back is his only chance," he told her softly. "He'll die if he stays here." Then he and the others stepped away to give Pocahontas and John a moment alone.

Pocahontas kneeled beside John Smith. Suddenly, Meeko appeared beside her. He had something for her. Pocahontas couldn't believe her eyes.

"My mother's necklace!" The raccoon must have gathered up the pieces next to Kocoum's body and put them back together. Now it was like new.

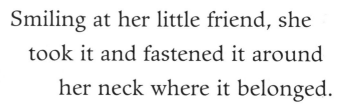

Smiling at her little friend, she took it and fastened it around her neck where it belonged. Then she turned her attention to John. He reached out to touch her face. "Come with me?" he asked.

It was the question Pocahontas had known was coming. She had been trying to decide what answer to give ever since she had learned that John needed to return to England to have his wound treated. But she still didn't know what to say. She glanced at her father, who had come with the others to see John off.

He smiled at her lovingly. "You must choose your own path," he told her.

Pocahontas looked at the two groups of people watching her. On one side of the clearing was the tribe

she had always known, and on the other was John's tribe, the Englishmen who had arrived so recently. Where did she belong? Which path was hers?

She knew her decision could be very important—not just for herself and John, but for their people as well. The two of them had helped stop the two groups from going to war, but that didn't mean the path to true and lasting peace would be an easy one. With John on his way back to England,

Pocahontas might be the best person to lead these separate peoples toward friendship. What would happen if she left now?

But what would happen if she stayed? She gazed at John. In the past few days, every angle of his face had become so familiar, so precious. How could she live without him? Was it selfish to want to remain at his side, no matter what the cost to anyone else?

Finally, she realized that her heart already knew the answer to that question. She gave her reply, knowing it was the true one. "I'm needed here," she told John softly.

"Then I'll stay with you," John said immediately.

"No," Pocahontas said, though her heart was breaking. "You have to go back."

"But I can't leave you," John told her.

"You never will," Pocahontas reminded him, thinking of the wise words he had spoken to her in the prison hut the night before. "No matter what happens, I will always be with you. Forever."

She kissed him one last time. Then she stood

and watched
as the
English
sailors lifted
the stretcher
and carried it to the
boat.

Powhatan approached
and put a hand on her shoulder. Pocahontas stood
with her father for a moment, taking strength from
his love.

Then she pulled away. As the English ship's
white sails caught the wind and the great vessel
moved out toward the sea, Pocahontas raced along
the shore, matching its progress, until she reached
the highest overlook. She stood there, her hair
blowing in the breeze, and watched as the strange
clouds carried John away.

On deck, John looked up and saw her. He raised
his hand, moving it in the circular motion that
Pocahontas had taught him.

Good-bye, he thought as he gazed up at her.

On the overlook, Pocahontas echoed the farewell gesture.

Good-bye, she thought as she watched the ship sail toward the rising sun on the far-off horizon.

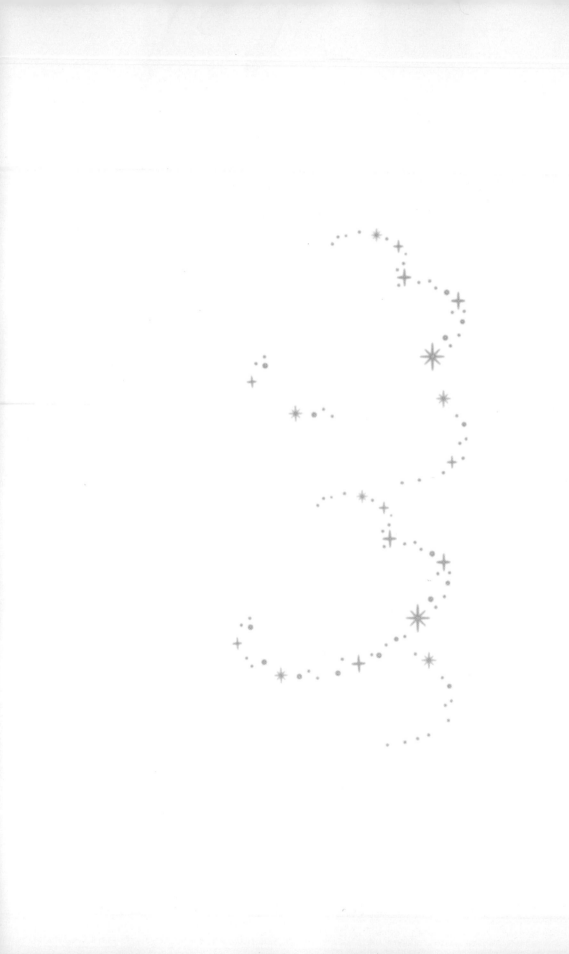

THE STORY OF
Cinderella

HOPES AND DREAMS

It was almost dawn, and the sky over the horizon was beginning to change color. Cinderella was fast asleep in her room in the tower of the château where she lived with her stepmother, Lady Tremaine, and two stepsisters, Anastasia and Drizella. Her lovely face wore a happy smile, for she was dreaming of her childhood—back to the time when her dear father was still alive.

The house had been filled with love and laughter in those days. But there had always been a touch of sadness as well. Cinderella barely remembered her

mother, but she knew her father had missed his wife very much.

Sometimes Cinderella would see him gazing down at the pocket watch that her mother had given him the last Christmas they had spent together. "Are you feeling sad, Father?" Cinderella would ask, tucking her small hand into his.

He would always smile at the question. "How could I be sad?" he would ask as he swung her up into his arms. "I have the most beautiful little girl in the world as my daughter!"

Cinderella would hug him tightly. She adored everything about her father—his bright smile, his elegant clothes, his friendly manner, his handsome mustache.

In turn, the kind gentleman doted on his daughter. He provided her with the finest of everything, from clothes to toys to tutors. He often took her for carriage rides to see the King's palace, or to have a picnic by the river. He spent hours pushing her on the swing in the garden, telling jokes until she was giggling so hard she could hardly hold on to the swing's ropes. She couldn't imagine a better life than living with him in the château.

But her father wasn't so sure that their life was truly complete. He felt that his daughter needed a mother's care. That was the reason he proposed marriage to a local widow, Lady Tremaine. She was a handsome woman from a good family, with two young daughters of her own—he was certain she would be the perfect stepmother for Cinderella.

"I think this is best for all of us, my dear," Cinderella's father told her. "You will have a mother again. And little Anastasia and Drizella will be the sisters you never had. How does that sound?"

"Wonderful, Father," Cinderella replied.

Though she knew she would have to get used to sharing her dear father with the newcomers, Cinderella really didn't mind the idea of the marriage. She hoped that having a new wife would make her father less lonely. Perhaps it would even make her own life better.

At first, that wish seemed to come true.

"What a beautiful child!" Lady Tremaine cooed upon meeting her new stepdaughter for the first time. "Such lovely golden hair, and such a pleasant face! Why, I don't remember ever meeting a young lady so charming."

"Thank you," Cinderella responded politely, curtsying just as her father had taught her. She noticed that Anastasia and Drizella were scowling at her, but she didn't worry about that. She was sure they would all be the best of friends before long.

For a while, life at the château was as pleasant and calm as ever. At first, Cinderella tried to befriend her new stepsisters. But Anastasia and Drizella were more interested in shopping for new dresses or gossiping about the goings-on at the King's palace than they were in playing in the garden with Cinderella. And so Cinderella continued playing alone or with her father. But even though Cinderella's new stepsisters were rather foolish and vain, their mother always treated her stepdaughter kindly. So Cinderella was happy.

Everything changed

the day that Cinderella's father died unexpectedly. It was only then that Lady Tremaine's true nature was revealed. Freed from her husband's watchful eye, she showed herself to be cold, cruel, and bitterly jealous of Cinderella's sweetness and beauty. She was determined to provide the best life for her own daughters, but their awkward manners and homely appearance were only magnified beside Cinderella's charms. So Lady Tremaine did all she could to dull those charms. She forced Cinderella to dress in plain peasants' clothes, live in a tiny, drafty room at the top of the tower, and wait on her stepfamily hand and foot, night and day.

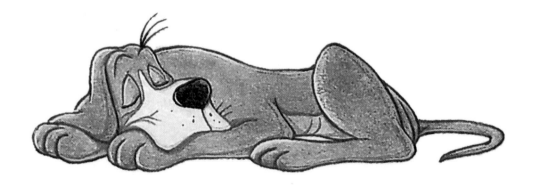

Sometimes Cinderella felt she had no friends left in the world, aside from her father's old dog, Bruno, and the little mice that lived in the walls of the house. Still, she never lost her kind, generous nature. And she never gave up her dreams of being happy again someday.

MORNING CHORES

A maidservant's day begins early, and that was what Cinderella had become—a maidservant in her own home. Awakening to the sweet songs of the birds outside her window, Cinderella yawned and stretched.

"Cinderella!" one little bird chirped.

The other flew through the open window and perched on the bed. "Cinderella!" it twittered.

Cinderella sat up, smiling at the birds. She scolded them playfully for spoiling her pleasant dream. The birds chirped back in protest and flew over to the window to show her the rising sun.

"Yes, I know it's a lovely morning," Cinderella told them, reaching back to undo her long, blond hair from its nighttime braid. "But it was a lovely dream, too."

Still, she knew that morning had to begin sometime, and it was nice to wake up to the beautiful voices of songbirds. In return, she sang to the little birds—as well as some mice that crept out of their holes to listen—as she brushed her hair.

The toll of a clock interrupted her sweet song. Cinderella looked out her window, which framed a view of the King's palace in the distance, including the clock tower.

Cinderella frowned slightly. "Oh, that clock," she said. "Old killjoy! Come on, get up, you say. Time to start another day."

The mice and birds watched sympathetically as Cinderella got out of bed and slipped on her shoes. She looked at them with a wistful smile.

"Even *he* orders me around," she said, gesturing to the clock. "Well, they can't order me to stop dreaming."

Still humming under her breath, Cinderella went about her morning routine. With a little help from her animal friends, she made the bed and got dressed. The birds tied a clean apron around her waist, Cinderella pulled back her hair in a tidy ribbon, and then she was ready to start the day.

In truth, Cinderella had never liked to sit around

with nothing to do, and she was always happy to keep busy. Deep down, the house still felt like home, and she didn't mind doing her part to take care of it. But why did she have to do everything? Why did Anastasia and Drizella have new gowns every season, while Cinderella was forced to make do with a few worn old garments? Why did the sisters spend their days with music lessons and needlepoint, while Cinderella spent hers preparing meals, doing laundry, and scrubbing floors?

Still, she tried not to think about such things too much. She had learned long ago that it was easier to do as she was told rather than resist her lot in life. When the chores were done promptly and well, her

stepfamily left her alone—usually. They were busy enough with their own problems. Anastasia and Drizella had reached a marriageable age, and Lady Tremaine was determined to find them suitable husbands. It wasn't an easy task, however. The two girls had grown from awkward, demanding, and unpleasant little girls into awkward, demanding, and unpleasant young women. Was it any wonder that suitors were nowhere to be found?

Still, Lady Tremaine refused to give up, doing all

she could to make her daughters more eligible, from hiring the finest tailors to make their clothes to teaching them the arts and skills young ladies of their class should know.

Cinderella made her way down the winding tower staircase to the second-floor hallway, opening the drapes to let in the morning sunlight. She moved as quietly as possible, knowing that her stepmother and stepsisters were still sleeping.

Tiptoeing to one of the doors in the hall, she cracked it open. Inside, her stepmother slept in a huge canopy bed. Beside the bed was an elaborate little bed where Lady Tremaine's fat black cat, Lucifer, slept. He was curled up there now, snoring contentedly.

"Here, kitty, kitty," Cinderella called softly.

Lucifer heard her. Opening his sly green eyes, he looked at the girl in the doorway. He stood, stretched—and lay down again with his back to her.

Cinderella frowned. It was easy to lose patience

with the stubborn, selfish cat. "Lucifer!" She snapped. "Come *here*!"

The cat scowled. But he knew better than to disobey—at least before breakfast. Jumping down from his bed, he slunk out the door after Cinderella.

"I'm sorry if Your Highness objects to an early breakfast," Cinderella told him as she led the way toward the stairs. "It's certainly not my idea to feed you first."

Downstairs, she poured a bowl of milk for the cat  and greeted Bruno the dog, who was sleeping on the kitchen rug. Then she walked outside to the stable yard.

"Breakfast time, everybody up!" she called out. "Hurry! Hurry!"

She tossed out grain for the chickens. The mice popped out of their holes, and songbirds fluttered down from the eaves, eager for their share. Cinderella always made sure there was extra food for her little friends, even though she knew her stepmother wouldn't approve. Sometimes it was convenient to be the only one who paid attention to the workings of the household!

Meanwhile, Lucifer had left his breakfast and was stalking one of the mice, a chubby little fellow named Gus. The cat watched, his tail twitching, as Gus struggled to pick up several kernels of corn and carry them back to his hole. Finally, Lucifer pounced, trapping Gus behind a broom in the corner. Aha! He had the mouse right where he wanted him. . . .

But the other mice weren't going to let Lucifer

catch their friend. When they pushed over the broom, it conked Lucifer on the head as it fell. That gave Gus enough time to race inside and hide under one of the teacups Cinderella had set out for breakfast.

Cinderella didn't notice the cat's antics. She was too busy worrying about the time as she tried to get everything done. It was getting late—if she didn't hurry with the breakfast, her stepfamily would wake up before she got there, and then—

"CINDERELLA!"

"All right, all right!" Cinderella raced over to the table. "Goodness, morning, noon, and night . . ."

"CINDERELLA!" another shrill voice rang out.

"Coming, coming," Cinderella muttered, though she knew her stepmother and stepsisters couldn't hear her. Gathering up the three breakfast trays, she headed up the stairs.

A Busy Morning

As Cinderella entered the first room in the upstairs hallway, she didn't realize that poor little Gus was still hiding under one of the cups on her trays.

"Good morning, Drizella," Cinderella greeted her sleepy stepsister pleasantly. "Sleep well?"

Drizella responded with a grunt. "As if you cared!" she added crossly. Then, she pointed to a large pile of wrinkled clothes on the floor. "Take that ironing and have it back in an hour. One hour. Do you hear?"

Cinderella set down one of the trays and picked up the clothing with her free hand. "Yes, Drizella," she said with a sigh.

She moved on to the next doorway. Once again, she walked inside and set down one of the breakfast trays.

"Good morning, Anastasia," she said politely.

"Well, it's about time!" Anastasia responded in a huff. "Don't forget the mending. And don't be all day getting it done, either!"

"Yes, Anastasia." Once again, Cinderella exchanged the tray for a basket of clothes. Then she left and headed for her stepmother's bedroom.

Lady Tremaine was sitting up in bed, waiting for her breakfast. Cinderella hesitated in the doorway, a little intimidated by her stepmother's stern expression.

"Well, come in, child," Lady Tremaine said. "Come in."

"Good morning, Stepmother," Cinderella said softly.

Lady Tremaine didn't return the greeting. "Pick up the laundry and get on with your duties," she said coldly.

"Yes, Stepmother," Cinderella said, setting down the final tray and picking up a third basket of clothes.

As she returned to the hall, a scream rang out from the second doorway. "Mother! Oh, Mother!" Anastasia screeched.

A moment later Anastasia burst into the hall, still dressed in her nightgown. She pointed an accusing finger at Cinderella.

"*You* did it!" she shrieked. "You did it on purpose! A big ugly mouse under my teacup!" She raced into her mother's room.

Cinderella immediately looked for the cat. She spotted him crouched near the doorway. "All right, Lucifer," she said. "What did you do with him?"

She reached down and picked up the cat, releasing Gus, who had been trapped under Lucifer's paws. The little mouse scooted away between Cinderella's

legs, heading for the nearest mouse hole, where he celebrated his freedom with his friends.

But Cinderella knew there was more to come. Sure enough, her stepmother's voice rang out a moment later—"Cinderella!"

Cinderella reluctantly returned to her stepmother's room. Anastasia and Drizella smirked as she entered.

"Are *you* going to get it!" Anastasia taunted.

Cinderella tried to explain that she hadn't hidden

the mouse there on purpose, but her stepmother wouldn't listen. Instead, she punished Cinderella by assigning her extra chores.

"The large carpet in the main hall—" she said with a hiss. "Clean it! And the windows, upstairs and down—wash them! Oh, yes, the tapestries and the draperies—"

"But I just finished—" Cinderella interrupted in protest.

Lady Tremaine didn't let her continue. "Do them again!" she cried. "And don't forget the garden, then scrub the terrace, sweep the halls and the stairs, clean the chimneys, and of course there's the mending and the sewing and the laundry."

Cinderella slumped under the weight of her stepmother's words. How could one person be expected to do so much? But she didn't argue. She knew it wouldn't do any good. Instead, she got to work.

It wasn't easy getting everything done, especially when her stepsisters kept interrupting with extra tasks. As Cinderella was sweeping the kitchen floor,

Anastasia burst in. She was holding her embroidery hoop. "Cinderella, these dumb old threads keep getting tangled," she complained. "Fix them for me!"

Cinderella sighed and reached out for the hoop. It wasn't that she minded helping—she knew that Anastasia was hopeless with a needle. But she would have minded less if her stepsister ever said a simple "please" or "thank you."

"Here you go," she said, quickly untangling the threads. "If you hold them to one side with your free hand, they shouldn't get tangled as easily."

Anastasia grabbed back the hoop. "I certainly don't need any tips from *you*," she snapped. "What do you know about embroidery? Or anything that has to do with being a proper lady?"

Turning up her nose, Anastasia stalked out of

the room. Cinderella merely sighed and went on with her work.

A little while later, Cinderella walked down the hall, carrying a load of laundry. She heard muttering coming out of the parlor. When she glanced inside, she saw that Drizella was standing at her easel with a paintbrush in her hand.

"What are you looking at?" Drizella said sourly. "Go away."

Cinderella started to move on. But suddenly Drizella called her back.

"Wait!" she yelled. "Get in here. I can't get the right shade of blue for the sky in my painting. Mix it for me— and make sure it's right."

"I'll try," Cinderella said, taking the tubes

of paint from her stepsister. She quickly added a bit of cloudy white, then a smidge of ocean blue, until she had created a perfect azure blue summer sky.

She dabbed a bit of the paint on Drizella's canvas and stared at it. Oh, to be out having a picnic under a clear blue sky, thought Cinderella.

Cinderella didn't realize her stepmother had entered the room until she heard her clear her throat. "That doesn't look like the laundry soap you're holding, Cinderella," Lady Tremaine said coolly.

Cinderella dropped the paint palette, startled. "I—I'm sorry, Stepmother," she stammered. "I was just—"

"She was just trying to ruin my painting!" Drizella interrupted. Snatching the canvas off the easel, she shoved it in front of her mother. "See? She smudged up the whole sky! It will never look right now!"

"Never mind, Drizella," Lady

Tremaine said. "I'll see that Cinderella works off the cost of a new canvas. But now, it's time for your music lesson. Come along."

"Oh, Mother," Drizella whined. "Can't we just skip music lessons today?"

Lady Tremaine frowned. "Not if you want to become a proper young lady, suitable for a rich husband to marry," she said. "Now come along—let's find your sister."

As they swept out of the room, Cinderella bent to clean up the paint. She hated her stepsisters' music lessons—they filled the whole house with their screeching—but at least they would be busy for a while. Maybe now she could catch up on her chores.

A ROYAL INVITATION

A few minutes later, Anastasia and Drizella were in the music room in the middle of their lesson. Anastasia blew a shrill, off-key tune on the flute, while Drizella attempted to sing along. Their mother accompanied their song on the piano.

Cinderella winced as she listened from the hallway, where she was scrubbing the marble floor. Who knew two people could hit so many wrong notes in such a short period of time?

Still, she managed to recognize the song her

stepsisters were trying to perform. It was one of her favorites—her father had often asked her to sing it for him. Cinderella hummed along, her melodious voice mingling with the tuneless screeches coming from the music room.

She scrubbed in time to the song. Somehow, the music seemed to make the work go faster. Soap bubbles floated up from her bucket, filling the air with their bright, weightless shapes, catching the light and reflecting beautiful rainbows of color.

Cinderella could see her own reflection in them—a girl in an apron, on her hands and knees,  scrubbing the floor. Soon, she started to daydream—she was dressed in a beautiful gown adorned with sparkling jewels, dancing beneath a canopy of stars. . . .

Then the pleasant dream burst just as suddenly as one of the bubbles when she noticed Lucifer crossing the room. His muddy feet left dirty tracks all over her nice clean floor. The cat paused and glanced at her with a smug, satisfied look.

"You mean old thing!" Cinderella cried. "I'm going to have to teach you a lesson." She chased the cat out of the room with her broom.

Just then, Cinderella heard a knock at the door. Before she could open the door, she heard a voice from the other side.

"Open in the name of the King!"

The King! Cinderella was surprised and curious. She swung open the door and saw a smartly dressed messenger standing outside. He held out an envelope sealed with red wax.

"An urgent message from His Imperial Majesty," the messenger announced.

Cinderella curtsied as

she accepted the letter. "Thank you," she told the messenger.

Then she shut the door and looked at the envelope. What could the message be? She couldn't imagine, but it was wonderfully exciting to receive such a letter!

Deciding that something this important shouldn't wait, she rushed to the music room and knocked on the door.

"Yes?" her stepmother's voice snapped from within.

Cinderella entered the room, still holding the royal letter.

"Cinderella!" Lady Tremaine said with a frown. "I've warned you never to interrupt us."

 "But this just arrived from the palace," Cinderella told her.

"From the palace?" Drizella exclaimed, rushing toward Cinderella. "Give it here!"

Anastasia was right beside her. She shoved her

sister out of the way and snatched the letter. "Let me have it!" she cried.

"No!" Drizella wailed. "It's mine! You give that back!"

Lady Tremaine stepped forward. "*I'll* read it," she announced, taking the letter from her daughters. As all three girls watched, she opened the envelope and scanned the letter. "Well," she said. "There's to be a ball."

"A ball!" Anastasia and Drizella cried in delight.

"In honor of His Highness, the Prince," Lady Tremaine went on. "And by royal command, every eligible maiden is to attend!"

"Hey, that's us!" Drizella exclaimed.

Anastasia nodded. "And I'm *so* eligible!"

Cinderella stood dumbfounded as her stepsisters continued to ooh and aah over the news. A ball? She knew of the prince, of course. He had been traveling recently, but she had overheard her stepsisters gossiping and knew that he was due to return to the kingdom any day now. She had also heard them say that the old King was eager to see his only son settled down and married as soon as possible.

Cinderella had heard that the Prince was very handsome, and very kind. What would it be like to meet him, perhaps even dance with him? She couldn't imagine it, and

until a moment ago wouldn't have dared to try. But the letter had said *every* eligible maiden. . . .

"Why," she cried, "that means I can go, too!"

Drizella laughed. "Ha!" she exclaimed. "Her, dancing with the Prince?"

Anastasia gave a mock bow, pretending to be Cinderella. "I'd be honored, Your Highness. Would you mind holding my broom?"

With that, she and Drizella burst into scornful laughter. Cinderella frowned.

"Well, why not?" Cinderella asked. "After all, I'm still a member of the family. And it says, by royal command, every eligible maiden is to attend."

Her stepmother glanced down at the letter, her face impassive. "Yes, so it does," she said. "Well, I see no reason why you can't go." She looked at Cinderella, ignoring her own daughters' expressions of dismay. "*If* you get all your work done."

"Oh, I will!" Cinderella cried, hardly believing her good luck. "I promise!" She dashed toward the door, eager to get started so there would be no chance of missing out on the royal ball.

"*And*," her stepmother cautioned, "if you can find something suitable to wear."

Cinderella beamed at her. "I'm sure I can." She still had a trunk of her mother's old dresses up in her tower room. Surely, there would be something in there that would be suitable. "Oh, thank you, Stepmother!"

THE PERFECT GOWN

Even though there were still plenty of chores to be done, Cinderella couldn't resist hurrying up to her room to look in her mother's old trunk. She opened it and dug through the contents. Just as she remembered, there were several dresses inside—including a beautiful pink-and-white ballgown. It was a bit out of style, but the fabric was clean and in good condition.

She swung the dress around to show it to her little mouse friends, who had gathered nearby to watch. Holding it up to herself, she smiled at them.

"Isn't it lovely?" she said. "It was my mother's." She turned and pulled the gown onto the dressmaker's dummy standing against a wall in the room.

 "Well, maybe it is a little old-fashioned," Cinderella added. "But I'll fix that."

Cinderella had always been quick and skilled with a needle and thread. Recently, she had been forced to use her skills to maintain the wardrobes of her stepmother and stepsisters. All that practice had made her fingers even more agile and swift. Now, finally, she would have a chance to sew for herself!

 She grabbed her sewing basket. There was a book inside that showed all the latest fashions. "There ought to be some good ideas in here," she murmured happily.

Flipping through the pages, Cinderella found exactly what she wanted. "This one!" she cried.

The mice looked at the picture. They chattered excitedly, approving of her choice.

"I'll have to shorten the sleeves," Cinderella mused, as she stood up and started dancing around her room. "I'll need a sash—a ruffle—and something for the collar, and then I'll—"

"Cinderella!"

The distant cry interrupted her thoughts. She frowned in the direction of the door. "Oh, now what do they want?" she exclaimed.

"Cinderella! Cinderella!"

Cinderella sighed and touched the soft fabric of the dress. "Oh, well," she said. "Guess my dress will just have to wait."

As she hurried out of the room, the mice chattered amongst themselves. Though Cinderella didn't seem to realize it, they could see what was happening. Cinderella's stepmother claimed she would let her stepdaughter attend the ball—*if* her chores were finished and her dress was ready. But the mice were sure that Lady Tremaine would never really allow Cinderella to go to the ball. She would be too likely to outshine her plain stepsisters! Instead, the mice were certain that Lady Tremaine planned to pile on the chores until there was no time left for Cinderella's own sewing.

It just wasn't fair! The mice were determined to help their friend if it were at all possible.

And they had a very good idea about how they could do it. . . .

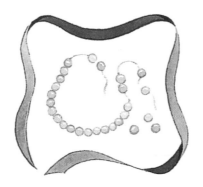

GETTING READY

When Cinderella returned, Anastasia and Drizella were already busy choosing their outfits for the ball. Somehow, though, none of their gowns seemed to be suitable. And as usual, that meant more mending, washing, and sewing for Cinderella.

"Cinderella, take my dress!" Drizella ordered, tossing a gown at her stepsister.

Anastasia rushed over with an armful of clothes. "Here, mend the buttonholes," she said, adding to Cinderella's load.

"And press my skirt," Drizella continued, piling on more. "And mind the ruffles, you're always tearing them!"

"And Cinderella," Lady Tremaine added, "when you're through, and before you begin your regular chores, I have a few little things . . ."

Cinderella felt her heart sink as she added up all the time it would take to do the things her stepfamily was demanding. How was she supposed to finish all these extra chores and still have time to prepare for the ball herself?

Unfortunately, she didn't have any choice but to

obey. She would just have to work as quickly as possible and hope for the best. "Very well," she whispered, turning away.

She spent the rest of the day rushing from the laundry room to the kitchen, back to the laundry room to the barn as fast as her legs would carry her! She hemmed her stepsisters' gowns, fixed their lunch, and rescrubbed the floor—thanks to Lucifer. The more chores she finished, the more it seemed she still had left to do. She didn't entirely give up hope until the sun set and she heard the clip-clop of horses' hooves outside.

Glancing out a window, she saw a fine carriage pulling up to the house. Lady Tremaine had hired it to pick up the family and drive them to the palace for the ball. Trying not to let her disappointment show on her face, Cinderella knocked on the door of the room where her stepmother was helping her daughters get dressed.

"The carriage is here," she said, without looking her stepmother in the eyes. How naive she had been! She had truly believed that her stepmother wanted to let her go. When in fact, she realized now, there had never really been any chance at all.

"Why, Cinderella!" Lady Tremaine feigned surprise. "You're not ready, child."

"I'm not going." Cinderella stared straight ahead. Whatever she did, she would not cry in front of them. She would never let them see how much they'd hurt her.

"Oh, what a shame," Lady Tremaine responded smoothly as her daughters smirked at each other. "But of course, there will be other times, and—"

"Yes," Cinderella cut off her stepmother's words. She couldn't stand to listen anymore. And she certainly didn't want to hang around and watch her stepfamily set out for the ball. "Good night."

It took all of her energy to drag herself up the stairs to her attic room. Instead of enjoying a wonderful, magical evening, dancing at the ball, talking to people, maybe even meeting the Prince, she was doomed to another lonely night in the attic, with only the mice as company. It wasn't fair! If her father were still alive . . .

But no. She couldn't think about that, or she really would break down and cry. That part of her life—the happy part—had ended long ago. She had no choice but to accept it.

Closing the door behind her without lighting the lamp, she wandered across the room toward the window. In the deepening twilight, the palace shone like a shimmering jewel lit from within.

"Oh, well, what's a royal ball?" she murmured, trying to make herself feel better. "After all, I suppose it would be frightfully dull. And—and—boring. And—and—" She sighed, giving in to the urge to feel sorry for herself. "—and completely wonderful."

 Seconds later, she turned and gasped in amazement. Her dress! But how—who—?

The gown was hanging from her dressing screen. The skirt had been draped with a silk sash and adorned with bows and ruffles. The sleeves had been shortened to look more stylish. Another bow decorated the neckline, which was now trimmed in lovely pink ribbon. It was beautiful!

"Surprise!" the mice cried in their squeaky voices. They jumped up and down, very pleased with their efforts. It had been difficult finding all the trimmings—especially when Lucifer could be lurking around any corner. But it was all worth it to see the amazed expression on Cinderella's face.

"Why, I—I never dreamed—it's such a surprise!" she stammered, grabbing the dress and holding it up, admiring it in the mirror. "How can I ever—why—oh, thank you so much!"

There was no time to say anything more. Cinderella quickly changed into the beautiful gown and ran a brush through her blond hair. The mice helped fasten a string of beads around her neck. It was the perfect finishing touch!

Then Cinderella raced down the stairs, calling "thank you" to her little friends over and over again. Soon she was dashing into the hall. Her stepsisters and stepmother were preparing to head outside, where the coach was waiting.

"Now remember," Lady Tremaine was telling her daughters. "When you're presented to His Highness, be sure to—"

"Wait!" Cinderella cried, interrupting. "Please, wait for me!"

She skidded to a stop in front of her family. Beaming, she spun around to show off her dress.

"Isn't it lovely?" she said breathlessly. "Do you like it? Do you think it will do?"

For a moment, Anastasia looked stunned. Then she looked angry. "Cinderella!" she cried.

Drizella joined in. "Mother," she whined, "she can't!"

"Girls, please." Lady Tremaine silenced her daughters with a look. "After all, we did make a

bargain, didn't we, Cinderella? And I never go back on my word."

As Anastasia and Drizella pouted, their mother peered more closely at Cinderella's dress. Cinderella smiled uncertainly. Shouldn't they be leaving? She didn't want to be late to the ball. But she remained silent under her stepmother's scrutiny.

"Hmm," Lady Tremaine said after a second. "How very clever, these beads." She touched the necklace Cinderella was wearing. "They give it just the right touch." She turned and glanced pointedly at her daughters. "Don't you think so, Drizella?"

"No, I don't," Drizella began angrily. "I think she's—" Finally getting a good look at the beads, she interrupted herself with a gasp of annoyance. She had just recognized the necklace as one she had discarded earlier that day. "Oh, why you little thief! They're my beads! Give them here!"

Cinderella gasped as her stepsister grabbed at the beads, ripping them off her neck. "Oh, no!" she cried.

"Oh, and look!" Anastasia exclaimed. "That's my

sash!" Darting forward, she tore the sash right off the front of Cinderella's dress.

"Oh, stop! Please!" Cinderella was horrified—she didn't know where to turn, what to do. How could they be so cruel? She tried to get away, but it was no use. Her stepsisters continued ripping her beautiful dress until it was in tatters.

Finally, Lady Tremaine spoke up. "Girls," she

scolded. "That's quite enough. Hurry along now—both of you. I won't have you upsetting yourselves."

Anastasia and Drizella obeyed, stepping haughtily out the door. Lady Tremaine followed, pausing just long enough to glance down at Cinderella, who was standing, staring down at the remains of her gown in shock.

"Good night," Lady Tremaine said pleasantly before exiting after her daughters.

As soon as she was alone, Cinderella broke down, burying her face in her hands. She raced outside, hardly knowing where she was going. She just wanted to get away—away from

this house, from her terrible stepfamily, her awful life. How had she ended up so miserable? She had tried to be a good person, to remain cheerful. She had tried to hold on to her dreams. But what good had it done, after all?

Reaching the garden, she collapsed against a bench and sobbed. Finally, after all these years, they had done it. They had truly broken her spirit.

BIBBIDI-BOBBIDI-BOO

For several long moments, Cinderella wept hopelessly. For once, she couldn't even imagine feeling happy again. She couldn't find a way to believe that things would get better.

"It's just no use," she whispered aloud. "No use at all. I can't believe—not anymore. There's nothing left to believe in—nothing!"

"Nothing, my dear?" a friendly voice asked.

Cinderella paused between sobs. Who had spoken? She'd thought she was all alone here in the garden. Suddenly, she realized that her head was no longer resting on the cold, stone bench, but was cradled in a soft, comfortable lap.

"Oh, now, you don't really mean that," the voice went on.

"Oh, but I do," Cinderella said, looking up into the kind, wrinkled face of an older woman. The woman was dressed in a blue hooded cape, and her eyes twinkled with wisdom and merriment.

"Nonsense, child," the woman responded cheerfully. "If you'd lost all your faith, I couldn't be here. And here I am!"

Cinderella wasn't sure what to think. Who was this woman? What was she doing here?

Meanwhile, the woman stood and helped Cinderella to her feet. "Come now, dry those tears," she said. "You can't go to the ball looking like that."

Cinderella glanced down at her torn dress. "The ball?" she said. "Oh, but I'm not . . ."

"Of course you are," the woman said briskly.

"But we'll have to hurry, because even miracles take a little time."

Cinderella blinked. "Miracles?"

The woman nodded, but she seemed a bit distracted. She glanced around. "What in the world did I do with that magic wand?" she murmured. "I was sure I—"

"Magic wand?" Cinderella repeated in amazement. Suddenly, everything was beginning to make sense—the old woman's sudden appearance here in the quiet garden, the twinkling, wise eyes, the magic wand . . . "Why, then you must be . . ."

The woman glanced at her. "Your Fairy Godmother, of course," she said, as if it were the most ordinary thing in the world. "Now, where is that wand—oh! I forgot. I put it away!"

She waved her hand in the air. Just like that, a wand appeared in a cloud of magical sparkles.

Cinderella gasped. So it was true! This really *was* her Fairy Godmother! She stood, speechless with wonder, as the woman gazed at her thoughtfully.

"Now, let's see," the Fairy Godmother murmured. "Hmm. I'd say the first thing you need is . . ."

Cinderella glanced down at her tattered dress.

". . . a pumpkin!" the Fairy Godmother cried.

"A pumpkin?" Cinderella said in confusion. She glanced over her shoulder at the pumpkin growing in the garden.

The Fairy Godmother ignored her consternation. She was tapping her chin, thinking hard. "Now, uh, the magic words," she mumbled. Suddenly, her face brightened. She cleared her throat and blurted out a bunch of strange syllables. Cinderella couldn't follow any of it except the last three words: "Bibbidi-bobbidi-boo!"

At the same time, the Fairy Godmother was

pointing her wand at the pumpkin. Magic sparkles shot toward the pumpkin—and with a shudder and a jump, it transformed into an elegant, gleaming coach!

"Oh!" Cinderella gasped. "It's beautiful!"

Several of the château's animals had crept out to see what was going on, including the mice, Bruno the dog, and the old horse from the stables. Even Lucifer had wandered out of the house to investigate the commotion.

Next the Fairy Godmother pointed at the coach. "Now, with an elegant coach like that, of course, we'll simply have to have . . ."

The horse stepped forward eagerly. But the Fairy Godmother wasn't looking at him. She pointed her wand again.

". . . mice!"

She waved her wand over a group of startled mice as she sang out the magic words once again. When she had finished, the plain little mice were transformed into four gleaming white horses!

Lucifer was so startled that he fell into the fountain with a splash.

"Ha-ha, poor Lucifer," Cinderella said with a smile.

"Serves him right, I'd say," the Fairy Godmother replied. "Now, where were we? Oh, goodness, yes. You can't go to the ball without a . . ."

Cinderella smiled. Maybe now she would take care of her dress!

". . . a horse!"

"Another one?" Cinderella said in surprise.

This time, the Fairy Godmother pointed her wand at the old horse. Tonight he wouldn't need to pull the coach—he would sit in the driver's seat and hold the reins! Soon he had been transformed into a uniformed coachman. A moment later, Bruno, too, had been called into service. He would be the footman.

With that done, the Fairy Godmother seemed satisfied.

"Well, well, hop in, my dear," she said to Cinderella. "We can't waste time."

"But, uh . . ." Cinderella gestured to her torn dress. "Don't you think my dress . . ."

"Yes, it's lovely, dear," the Fairy Godmother said distractedly. "Lov—" Suddenly she gasped. "Good heavens, child! You can't go in that!"

Cinderella sighed, smiled, and shook her head.

The Fairy Godmother got ready to go back to work. "Now, let's see, dear," she murmured, stepping toward Cinderella. "Your size—and the shade of your eyes—something simple, but daring, too . . ."

She took a deep breath and, once more, said the magic words. Cinderella held her breath. She could feel magic flowing around her, and she could see it, too—twinkling like fireflies. She closed her eyes as it washed over her.

When she opened them again, she looked down and gasped. "Oh!" she cried. "It's a beautiful dress!"

And indeed it was. It was made of yards and yards of flowing silk the color of the clearest waters.

Long, white gloves covered her arms, and a blue band of silk adorned her upswept hair. White pearl earrings and a black velvet choker completed the outfit, along with a pair of delicate glass slippers perfectly molded to her dainty feet.

"It's like a dream!" Cinderella exclaimed, spinning and twirling and admiring her new gown. "A wonderful dream come true!"

Her Fairy Godmother smiled gently. "Yes, my child," she said. "But like all dreams, I'm afraid this can't last forever. You'll have only until midnight and then—"

"Midnight?" Cinderella interrupted happily. Midnight was still hours away. "Oh, thank you!"

"Oh, now, just a minute," her Fairy Godmother said more sternly. "You must understand, my dear, on the stroke of twelve the spell will be broken, and everything will be as it was before."

Cinderella stepped toward her, still smiling. "Oh, I understand," she assured her. "But it's more than I ever hoped for."

The Fairy Godmother relaxed and returned her smile. "Bless you, my child."

It was time to go. Cinderella lifted the hem of her skirt and hurried toward the coach. The footman held the door for her as she climbed inside. The horses snorted and moved off at the command of the coachman. Cinderella barely had time to wave her thanks to her Fairy Godmother before the coach moved off toward the palace. She was on her way!

It wasn't a long trip, and soon the coach was pulling up at the foot of the palace steps. Not even the palace guards, who had already seen the most beautiful and elegant young women in the kingdom pass them that night, could resist a second look at Cinderella in her stunning gown.

She climbed the steps and entered the ballroom.

It was crowded with elegantly dressed people. Cinderella gazed about in awe, not sure which way to go first—she had never been inside the palace before. As she stood there uncertainly, she glanced up and saw a young man striding toward her.

He stopped before her and bowed. Blushing slightly, she curtsied in return. She had never seen such a handsome young man. He was tall and dark

haired, with intelligent eyes and a courteous manner. It was the Prince.

The Prince reached for her hand and kissed it. "May I have this dance, miss?" he asked politely.

"Yes," Cinderella replied.

Cinderella didn't say another word. There was no need. The Prince led her toward the dance floor, and just like that, they were dancing.

The orchestra was playing a waltz. The Prince and Cinderella danced beautifully together as if they'd done so many times before. And indeed, something about the young man made Cinderella feel comfortable—as if they knew each other even without speaking.

Cinderella didn't notice her stepmother and stepsisters staring at her, trying to figure out why the lovely young lady in the elegant gown looked so familiar. She was completely unaware of the many other eyes on her as she danced. She was also completely unaware that the young man was the Prince.

So this is love, she thought with wonder as he

led her out into the palace garden. They continued to dance there, watched only by the stars in the sky overhead.

Finally growing tired, they stopped dancing and walked instead. Hand in hand, they wandered through the darkened gardens and over a footbridge that crossed a small, sparkling stream. They paused in the middle of the bridge, turning toward each other. Cinderella's heart swelled as they embraced.

As their lips touched, a sudden sound broke the silence of the garden.

Bong!

"Oh!" Cinderella cried, pulling back from the young man. "Oh, my goodness!"

"What's the matter?" the Prince asked.

Cinderella glanced at the clock tower as it let out another chime. "It's midnight!" she exclaimed. How could she have lost track of the time? How could she have forgotten her Fairy Godmother's warning?

"Yes, so it is." The young man looked confused. "But why . . . ?"

"Good-bye!" Cinderella cried, pulling away as the clock continued to chime. How many strikes had it been? She had to hurry, or her secret would be revealed! It had been such a perfect evening, and she just wanted to remember it that way.

The young man hurried after her, catching her by the hand. "Oh, no, wait!" he exclaimed. "You can't go now."

"Oh, I must," Cinderella insisted desperately, letting go of his hand. With every chime she grew more frantic. "Please, please, I must!"

"But why?" The Prince couldn't understand why the young woman was suddenly so eager to leave.

There was no time to explain the truth, even if she'd wanted to. She had to come up with a reason—it wasn't fair to let the young man wonder. "W-Well, I," she stammered, trying to think of an excuse. "The Prince! I—I haven't met the Prince!"

"The Prince?" the Prince repeated in surprise. "But didn't you know . . . ?"

The clock chimed again—time was running out!

"Good-bye!" Cinderella cried again, running away at last.

"Wait!" the young man's voice followed her. "Come back! Oh, please, come back! I don't even know your name. How will I find you?"

Cinderella hardly heard him. She didn't dare slow down or even look back. Gathering her skirts, she raced through the ballroom and across the grand entryway to the front steps. Her coach was at the bottom waiting for her. Maybe there was still time. . . .

As she raced down the steps, one of her glass slippers fell off. She paused and turned around to retrieve it, but before she could, she spotted a man in a palace uniform coming after her. "Mademoiselle," he called. "Just a moment!"

Now what? Cinderella

couldn't imagine what he wanted, but there was no time to find out. Leaving the glass slipper behind, she ran the rest of the way down the steps and leaped into her coach.

"Guards!" the man called. "Guards, follow that coach!"

Why were they chasing her? Cinderella had no idea. She didn't realize that the young man she'd spent the evening with was really the Prince, and that he was determined to  stop her from rushing away out of his life. All Cinderella knew was that the clock was nearing the last stroke of midnight.

Sure enough, one last *bong* rang out over the

kingdom. And with it, the magic spell ended. The galloping horses changed into running mice. The coachman and footman returned to their ordinary shapes as horse and dog. And Cinderella suddenly found herself sitting atop a pumpkin, wearing her old, ripped pink dress.

There was barely enough time to dash off the road and into hiding in the brush when the King's men galloped by in search of them. Their horses' hooves smashed the pumpkin into smithereens, but Cinderella and her animal friends escaped unhurt and unnoticed.

Finally, when the searchers had passed, Cinderella let out a sigh of relief and turned to her friends. "I'm sorry," she told them. "I—I guess I forgot about everything, even the time. But—but it was so wonderful!" She sighed happily, thinking back over the incredible evening. Her thoughts focused on the young man. She didn't even know his name, but she knew she would never forget him as long as she lived. "And he was so handsome—and then we danced—oh, I'm sure even the Prince himself couldn't have been more—"

Suddenly, one of the mice began chattering and pointing at Cinderella's foot. Looking down, Cinderella gasped in surprise. She was still wearing one of the glass slippers! It hadn't changed back to an ordinary shoe.

Cinderella smiled, guessing that this was a special gift from her Fairy Godmother. Now she would have a memento of this glorious evening. Even if nothing good ever happened to her again, she would always be able to look at this beautiful, perfect glass slipper and remember the most magical night of her life.

"Oh!" she cried, clutching the slipper to her chest. She smiled up at the sky, knowing somehow that her Fairy Godmother would be able to hear her. "Thank you! Thank you so much—for everything!"

THE ROYAL PROCLAMATION

T he next morning, a notice was posted in the town square:

Whereas the King desires a search be conducted throughout the kingdom in order to find that certain maiden whose foot shall fit a certain glass slipper; and Whereas said maiden is the one and only true love of our noble Prince, So Be It Proclaimed That, upon finding said maiden, His Royal Highness the Prince will humbly request her hand in marriage to rule with him as Royal Princess and future Queen.

The notice was marked with the official seal of the King. Lady Tremaine saw the posting and realized this could be the chance her daughters needed. She had been outraged that Anastasia and Drizella hadn't had even a moment to talk with and charm the Prince—that strange girl in the pale blue dress had monopolized his company all evening. It was outrageous!

But now, everything could be made right. All she had to do was make sure that one of the girls' feet fit into that slipper. . . .

"Cinderella!" she shouted as she entered the house. "Cinderella! Cinderella! Oh, where is that—"

"Here I am," Cinderella interrupted, appearing in the doorway.

"Oh!" Lady Tremaine was momentarily startled by Cinderella's sudden appearance. And what was that strange faraway expression on her face? But she didn't have time to worry about such things right now. "My daughters," she snapped. "Where are they?"

"I think they're still in bed," Cinderella responded rather dreamily.

Lady Tremaine frowned at her. "Oh," she said. "Oh, well, don't just stand there. Bring up the breakfast trays at once. Hurry!"

As Lady Tremaine rushed up the stairs toward her daughters' bedrooms, Cinderella wandered to the kitchen. She hummed softly while she prepared the breakfast trays. Somehow, even ordinary chores didn't seem so bad this morning. All she had to do was think about the night before and she was filled with happiness.

The only sad part was knowing she would probably never see that young man again. But she couldn't possibly complain about that. Just meeting him, spending that one glorious evening dancing with him, had been a dream come true. How could she ask for more than that?

Lifting the heavy trays, she headed upstairs, still

humming. She headed for Anastasia's bedroom, but even before she reached it, she could hear her stepmother talking to her daughters inside.

"Hurry now," she was exclaiming, her stern voice sounding excited. "He'll be here any minute!"

"Who will?" Drizella was standing in the doorway of her sister's room, looking sleepy.

"The Grand Duke!" Lady Tremaine responded impatiently. "He's been hunting all night for that girl."

Cinderella paused in the hallway, wondering what her stepmother was talking about.

"The one who lost her slipper at the ball last night," Lady Tremaine went on. "They say he's madly in love with her!"

"The Duke is?" Anastasia asked in confusion.

"No, no, no!" her mother exclaimed. "The Prince!"

Cinderella gasped. "The Prince!" she whispered. Suddenly, everything made sense. That handsome young man—the palace official chasing her—and now this.

Her whole body seemed to go numb. The Prince! In love with her! One of the breakfast trays slipped out of her hands and crashed to the floor.

The sudden noise attracted Lady Tremaine's attention. She glared at Cinderella. "You clumsy little fool. Clean that up, and then help my daughters dress."

"What for?" Drizella complained sourly.

Anastasia nodded. "If he's in love with that girl, why should we even bother?"

"Now you two listen to me," Lady Tremaine replied sharply. "There is still a chance that one of you can get him. No one—not even the Prince—knows who that girl is. The glass slipper is their only clue. The Duke has been ordered to try it on every girl in the kingdom, and if one can be found whom the slipper fits, then by the King's command, that girl shall be the Prince's bride."

Cinderella was listening as she cleaned up the fallen tray. She sat up straight in awe. "His bride," she whispered. It was such an amazing thought that she hardly dared to think it. That wonderful young man—the Prince!—wanted her to be his bride!

She was hardly aware that her stepsisters were gathering up their best clothes and piling them in her arms to launder and mend. She stared into space, still trying to take in the shock of this news. The Prince! She was in love with the Prince!

And he was in love with her!

Without realizing what she was doing, she let everything drop to the floor and, deaf to her stepsisters' protests, wandered off down the hall. She wanted to wash up before the Duke arrived. As she climbed the stairs toward her own room, she was still humming the chorus of a waltz she had danced to the night before.

Meanwhile Lady Tremaine was staring at her suspiciously.

"What's the matter with her?" Anastasia complained.

"Mother, did you see what she did?" Drizella added. "Why, I never saw—"

"Quiet!" her mother commanded. Recognizing the tune that Cinderella was humming, Lady Tremaine realized that her stepdaughter must have been at the ball. So that was why that lovely young lady had seemed so familiar last night. . . . She had no idea how Cinderella had done it, but she didn't plan to let her get away with it.

Leaving her daughters behind to gather up their clothes, Lady Tremaine crept up the stairs after Cinderella. When she reached the tower, she could hear the girl still humming and singing in her room. Her eyes narrowed as she watched her from the doorway.

Cinderella brushed her hair. As she gazed into the mirror, she caught a glimpse of her stepmother.

Lady Tremaine reached around the door and
took the key from the lock. Before Cinderella could
stop her, she slammed the door shut—and locked it
from the outside!

"No!" Cinderella cried, spinning around and racing for the door. "Please, you can't—you can't!"

But she had. The door was locked tight.

"Let me out!" Cinderella cried. Her words
turned into sobs as she realized what was

going on. Her stepmother meant to keep her locked up in the tower until the Duke had come and gone. She felt her dreams slipping away once again. "Let me out! You must let me out!"

The mice had seen the whole thing. Once again, they went to the aid of their dear friend Cinderella. . . .

The mice scurried downstairs through the walls. The key was in Lady Tremaine's pocket. Could they steal it back and free Cinderella? There wasn't much time—already the Duke's carriage was pulling up in front of the house.

In the parlor, Lady Tremaine felt very pleased with herself. That had been a close one—Cinderella had nearly ruined all her plans. But now it was just a matter of forcing that glass slipper onto one of her daughters' feet, and their future would be secured.

"Now remember," she warned her daughters as she got ready to open the door and admit the Duke, "this is your last chance. Don't fail me!"

Soon the Duke was calling for the glass slipper, which a footman brought to him, nestled on a silk pillow. He wasn't sure why he bothered—he had seen the lovely young woman the Prince was speaking to, and she had looked nothing at all like these two girls. Still, he had his orders—he was to try the slipper on every maiden's foot.

"Why, that's my slipper!" Drizella cried, reaching for it.

Anastasia pushed her aside. "It's my slipper!" she exclaimed.

"Girls! Girls! Your manners!" Lady Tremaine cried. She smiled at the Duke. "A thousand pardons, Your Grace." She was so busy imagining the grand life the three of them would soon be leading at the palace that she didn't notice when the mice formed a chain and lifted the key right out of her pocket!

The Duke read the proclamation, then announced that it was time to proceed with the fitting. He held out the slipper as Anastasia extended her large, knobby foot.

"There!" Anastasia cried, hoping against hope that the Duke wouldn't notice that the tiny slipper was dangling off her big toe. "I knew it was my slipper." She grimaced as the Duke gave her a skeptical look. "Oh, well, it may be a trifle snug today. You know how it is—dancing all night."

She struggled to shove the rest of her foot into the slipper, but it was no use. The slipper was much too small.

Then it was Drizella's turn. But her foot was no smaller or daintier than her sister's. She puffed and panted and labored to squeeze her foot into the slipper, but it was no use.

The Duke grabbed the slipper back before Drizella could damage it. He stood, preparing to move on to the next house.

"You are the only ladies of the household, I hope?" He corrected the slip of the tongue quickly. "I presume?"

Lady Tremaine's face was grim. "There's no one else, Your Grace."

"Quite so." The Duke put on his hat and turned toward the door. "Good day."

"Your Grace!" a new voice stopped him. "Your Grace!"

Cinderella raced down the stairs. The mice had done it—they had released her from her tower prison just in the nick of time!

"Please, wait!" Cinderella cried. "May I try it on?"

The Duke removed his hat again, stunned by the beauty of the simply dressed young girl hurrying toward him. Meanwhile, Lady Tremaine and her daughters were chattering their protests:

"Pay no attention to her. . . ."

"It's only Cinderella . . . our scullery maid. . . ."

But the Duke ignored them. He smiled at Cinderella, holding out his hand as she reached the bottom of the stairs.

"Come, my child," he told her kindly. He led her to a chair and gestured for the footman to bring the slipper.

But as the footman hurried toward him, Lady Tremaine made one last desperate attempt to foil Cinderella. She stuck out her walking stick and tripped the footman. He lurched forward, and the slipper flew off its pillow. It sailed through the air—and shattered into a thousand pieces against the hard marble floor.

The Duke gasped in horror. "Oh, no, no, no!" he cried, flinging himself to the ground and picking up the broken pieces. Now what would he do? Could he possibly put the slipper together again? "This is terrible," he moaned. "The King—what will he say? What will he do?"

Cinderella was still sitting in her chair. "Perhaps if it would help . . ." she began.

The Duke was still kneeling before the broken slipper. "No, no, nothing can help now, nothing!" he wailed.

Cinderella brought something out of her pocket and held it up. "But you see," she said, "I have the other slipper."

Both Lady Tremaine and the Duke froze in

shock—one horrified, one jubilant. The Duke was
the first to react.

He smiled and rushed toward the girl, grabbing the
second glass slipper and kissing it with relief. Then,
before anything else could happen, he
carefully slid the slipper onto the
girl's dainty foot.

It fit perfectly, as he had
known it would.

A Dream Come True

C inderella smiled at her reflection in the mirror. She could hardly believe that she was here in the palace, and that it was her wedding day. In just a few moments, she would be standing beside her true love—the Prince—and they would declare their eternal devotion to each other in front of the whole kingdom. It seemed almost too good to be true!

"Thank you," she said to the servants who were adjusting her veil. "Thank you so much!"

She stared again at her reflection. Her wedding

gown was beautiful—pure white, with long sleeves
and a full, sweeping skirt. Around her throat she
wore a slim black velvet ribbon just like the one she'd
worn the night she'd met her Prince.

At that moment, her Fairy Godmother appeared
beside her in the mirror. Her eyes were
twinkling.

"Oh!" Cinderella cried, turning to hug her. "I
was hoping you would come!"

"I wouldn't miss it for the world, child," her Fairy Godmother responded, squeezing her tightly. "You look marvelous! Simply beautiful."

"Thank you." Cinderella blushed. "Thank you for everything. I never dreamed anything so wonderful could ever happen to me."

Her Fairy Godmother winked. "Of course you did, my dear." She explained: "You've had your troubles—more than most people, I'd say—but through it all you never lost faith that things would get better. You never stopped believing in the future. That's the only way to find happiness, you know."

Cinderella smiled, realizing that her Fairy Godmother was right. Deep within her heart, she had kept right on wishing and dreaming and hoping, even when things looked their darkest.

Soon, a servant knocked on the door. The ceremony was about to begin. The Fairy Godmother disappeared as the other woman entered, but

Cinderella knew her Fairy Godmother would be watching from wherever she was.

The servant looked at the future princess and smiled. In her short time in the palace, Cinderella had already won the hearts of the entire staff with her pleasant and humble manner.

"Dear girl," the woman said kindly, "you are the most beautiful bride I have seen in all my seventy years. I hope you will also be the happiest."

"Thank you," Cinderella responded shyly. She knew the old woman's wish had already come true. No one could possibly be any happier than Cinderella was at this moment!

As she walked down the aisle a few minutes later, Cinderella saw many familiar faces in the crowd. The King was there, of course, beaming with pride at his handsome son and future daughter-in-law.

The Grand Duke and other officials were there as well.

Cinderella even spotted Gus and the other mice cheering her on, dressed up in tiny blue coats for the special occasion. She smiled at them, knowing that they were enjoying palace life just as much as she was. Not only were there much nicer scraps to steal from the palace kitchen but the mice no longer had to worry about escaping Lucifer's claws!

Thinking of the grumpy old cat reminded Cinderella of her stepfamily. She glanced around, but Lady Tremaine and her daughters were nowhere to be seen in the crowd. Cinderella felt a brief touch of regret. Her stepfamily still refused to accept her good fortune and share in her happiness. Cinderella had sent the Duke to their château with an invitation to the wedding. Even after all their years of

petty cruelty, she was willing to make amends. But clearly, her stepfamily had been unable to accept her kindness.

Still, Cinderella wouldn't let such thoughts dampen her joy on this wonderful day. All she could do was see that her stepfamily had enough money to get by from now on. The rest was up to them. They would have to find their own happiness, just as she had.

The ceremony flew by all too quickly. Soon, Cinderella found herself running down the steps, hand in hand with her new husband. Halfway down, one of her slippers fell off. Laughing, she paused to retrieve it. The Prince laughed, too, then led her the rest of the way down the stairs. At the bottom, a grand carriage was waiting to whisk them away on their honeymoon.

The entire kingdom had gathered outside the palace to see the happy royal couple. There were shouts of congratulations and cheers from all sides. Cinderella did her best to wave her thanks to every-

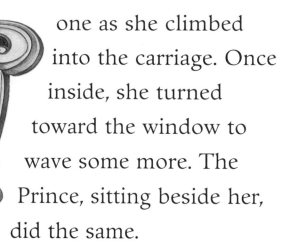

one as she climbed into the carriage. Once inside, she turned toward the window to wave some more. The Prince, sitting beside her, did the same.

"We're going to be very happy, you know," he whispered to her.

Cinderella turned and smiled at the Prince. "Oh, I know," she murmured. "I know."

The royal couple kissed as the carriage pulled away. Finally, Cinderella dared to believe that this was really happening. She had just married the man she loved, and now they were driving off to begin their life of happiness together.

All her dreams had finally come true.